*"You know as well as I do that the two of us can't be together. What in hell was Geraldine thinking?"*

Her blood simmering, Mercedes tossed her head, sending her thick hair rippling down her back. "She was thinking that we're two adults with a job to do. Not to claw and hiss at each other."

Gabe's eyelids lowered as his gaze settled on her lips. "Or to make love," he whispered hoarsely.

*Make love.*

She didn't know whether it was those two words or the low growl of his voice that sent a sultry shiver down her spine. Either way, she couldn't stop her body from gravitating toward his. "That—won't be on the agenda."

"Unless you want it to be."

Dear Reader,

Have you ever been betrayed by a friend, a loved one? I figure most all of us have at one time or another. It's a crushing, humiliating experience. One that's very hard to move past and forget.

When Mercedes Saddler comes home to the Sandbur after a long stint in the military, she's dealing with past betrayals that have made her sidestep the desire for love and family. But then she meets Gabe Trevino, the Sandbur's new horse trainer, and soon learns that he's not only hiding physical scars, but also scars hidden deep in his heart.

Sounds impossible for this pair to get together, doesn't it? But love is a powerful thing. Once it blooms, it gives us the strength and courage to trust again, to push aside our fears and reach for happiness.

I hope you enjoy reading how Mercedes and Gabe finally learn to open their hearts to each other!

God bless each trail you ride,

*Stella*

# HITCHED TO
# THE HORSEMAN

## *STELLA BAGWELL*

Silhouette®

## SPECIAL EDITION®

Published by Silhouette Books

**America's Publisher of Contemporary Romance**

SILHOUETTE BOOKS

ISBN-13: 978-0-373-24923-7
ISBN-10:  0-373-24923-3

HITCHED TO THE HORSEMAN

**Books by Stella Bagwell**

Silhouette Special Edition

*Found: One Runaway Bride* #1049
*\*Penny Parker's Pregnant!* #1258
*White Dove's Promise* #1478
*†Should Have Been Her Child* #1570
*†His Defender* #1582
*†Her Texas Ranger* #1622
*†A Baby on the Ranch* #1648
*In a Texas Minute* #1677
*†Redwing's Lady* #1695
*†From Here to Texas* #1700
*†Taming a Dark Horse* #1709
*†A South Texas Christmas* #1789
*†The Rancher's Request* #1802
*†The Best Catch in Texas* #1814
*†Having the Cowboy's Baby* #1828
*Paging Dr. Right* #1843
*†Her Texas Lawman* #1911
*†Hitched to the Horseman* #1923

Silhouette Books

The Fortunes of Texas
  *The Heiress and the Sheriff*

Maitland Maternity
  *Just for Christmas*

*A Bouquet of Babies*
  \*"Baby on Her Doorstep"

*Midnight Clear*
  \*"Twins under the Tree"

*Going to the Chapel*
  "The Bride's Big Adventure"

\*Twins on the Doorstep
†Men of the West

## STELLA BAGWELL

sold her first book to Silhouette in November 1985. Now, she still loves her job and says she isn't completely content unless she's writing. She and her husband live in Seadrift, Texas, a sleepy little fishing town located on the coastal bend. Stella says the water, the tropical climate and the seabirds make it a lovely place to let her imagination soar and to put the stories in her head down on paper.

She and her husband have one son, Jason, who lives and teaches high school math in nearby Port Lavaca.

To my husband, Harrell,
my very own horse trainer.
All my love.

## Chapter One

What the hell was he doing here?

Gabriel Trevino tilted the bottle of beer to his lips to hide his frown as his eyes cut across the sweeping lawn filled with people. Normally his social events consisted of sharing a beer with his buddies behind the bucking chutes at a local rodeo. This gathering at the Sandbur Ranch could hardly be compared to that sort of tobacco-spitting, curse-laden entertainment. Even the boring parties Sherleen had dragged him to during their ill-fated union paled in comparison to tonight's lavish celebration.

The best that money could buy.

The food, the drinks, the five-piece band, the women with hunks of diamonds glittering at their necks and wrists. Only in Texas, he thought wryly, could a woman justify wearing her best to an outdoor barbecue.

Leaning against the massive trunk of a live oak, he turned

his attention to the portable dance floor that had been erected several yards away from the house. Presently, it was crowded with couples. Some of them old, some young, all of them having a high old time kicking up their heels to the Cotton Eyed Joe.

"What's the matter, Gabe? Don't you like to dance?"

Glancing around, he saw Geraldine Saddler, the matriarch of the Sandbur, approaching him. The tall, elegant woman with silver hair hardly looked like a woman who knew how to burn a brand into a cowhide, but since he'd come to work here at the ranch two months ago, he'd seen her do things that would make even some cowhands squeamish.

"Sometimes," he replied.

Eyeing him keenly, she smiled. "Just not now?"

Embarrassed that his discomfort was showing, Gabe straightened away from the tree and turned to face her.

"It's enough for me just to watch, ma'am."

Kindness and grace emanated from Geraldine and for one brief moment, Gabe wondered what his mother's life would have been like if she'd been exposed to this sort of wealth, if she'd had a nice home, plenty of food and enough money to pay the bills with plenty left over for luxuries.

"This is the first party we've had since you arrived here on the ranch," Geraldine remarked. "I'd like to think you're enjoying yourself."

"Oh. Well, it's a real nice affair, Ms. Saddler. Real nice."

Looping her arm through his, she chuckled. "Come along, Gabe. I want to introduce you to someone."

Not about to offend her by protesting, Gabe allowed the woman to guide him through the milling throng of merrymakers until they reached the patio where several people were standing around in a circle.

Lex Saddler, Geraldine's son and the man who regulated

the cattle sales here at the Sandbur, was one of them. Apparently he'd just said something funny, because a tall, blond woman was laughing rowdily. She was wearing a skimpy white sundress with vivid tropical flowers splashed along the hem. The garment struck her long legs somewhere in the middle of her tanned thighs while the top was held up by tiny straps that could easily be snapped beneath the pressure of his fingers. Unlike most of the other young women present tonight, she wasn't stick-thin. She had enough flesh to fill out the sundress with delicious curves.

As Gabe and the boss lady drew nearer to the group, the blonde turned slowly toward them. Almost instantly, a faint look of unease crossed her features, as though seeing him with Geraldine was like spotting a wolf in a pen full of sheep.

"Mercedes, come here," Geraldine called to her. "I'd like for you to meet someone."

*Mercedes.* This was Geraldine's daughter, he realized. Lex and Nicci's sister. She was the reason hordes of guests had swarmed upon the Sandbur Ranch tonight. She was the reason he was standing here wishing like hell he was somewhere else.

Excusing herself from the intimate circle, the woman walked over to where they stood. Soft, expensive perfume drifted to his nostrils as he struggled to keep his eyes on her face, rather than the sensual curves of her body.

He sensed Geraldine releasing his arm as she quickly made introductions. "Gabe, this is my daughter, Mercedes. And this is Gabriel Trevino. He's our new head horse trainer here on the ranch."

The woman was young. Much younger than Gabe's thirty-five years, he decided. But her dark blue eyes were eyeing him with a shrewd perception that implied she was mature beyond her years. Pure attraction for the sultry beauty standing before him twisted in his gut.

Tilting the brim of his straw cowboy hat, he inclined his head toward her and she responded by thrusting her hand out to him.

"Nice to meet you, Mr. Trevino."

Closing his hand around hers, he was surprised by her firm shake, the warmth of her fingers.

"My pleasure, Ms. Saddler."

Sure. He was feeling as pleased as a bull in a squeeze chute, Mercedes thought. The man was bored. She could see it all over his face. But oh, my, what a face. Strong square jaw, dimpled chin and a Roman nose that had arrogance written all over it. Storm cloud-gray eyes peered at her from beneath heavy black brows. And his mouth—well, it would have looked delicious if a smile had been curving the corners. Instead, the firm slash was bracketed with faint lines of disdain.

Much to her dismay, her curiosity was instantly aroused by his reaction and she continued to hold on to his hand. Partly because she found touching him pleasant, and partly because she knew it was making him even more uncomfortable.

"So you've taken over Cousin Cordero's job," she mused aloud. "How do you like it here on the Sandbur?"

His dark gray gaze momentarily slanted over to Geraldine, and Mercedes watched a genuine smile cross her mother's face. Apparently she considered this man more than just a hired horse trainer. But then Geraldine was the sort of person who'd always gotten close to her employees, who always focused on the good in people rather than their faults.

"I like it," he answered quietly. "Your family has been very generous and gracious to me."

There wasn't anything particularly distinctive about his voice, yet something about the gravelly tones left her feeling a bit breathless. Silly, she told herself. She wasn't about to give in to the sensation. The feeling would pass. Just like this man would no doubt eventually move on from the Sandbur. He sure didn't look like the establishing-roots kind.

"The Sandbur has always had an excellent *remuda*," Mercedes remarked. "I'm sure you'll enjoy working with them. And Uncle Mingo is a legend in the cutting-horse business."

"Your uncle is a very special man," he agreed.

Her fingers were beginning to sweat against his, forcing Mercedes to drop his hand. As Mercedes shifted her weight on high-heeled sandals, Geraldine began to speak.

"Gabe has worked for years with problematic horses," she proudly explained. "He gets them over difficult issues and teaches them to bond with man rather than fight him. We're very lucky to have Gabe with us."

So the man could tame a wounded beast. Wonder what he did for women, Mercedes asked herself as her gaze slid to his ring finger. Empty. No surprise there. Obviously there wasn't a woman in the background to smooth out his rough edges. He looked as tough as nails and as wild as a rangy mustang.

"That must be challenging," she said to Gabe.

A faint smile curved the corners of his rough-hewn lips, and Mercedes was both ashamed and shocked at the little thrill of attraction that suddenly zipped through her. He was pure male animal. Any woman would be attracted, she tried to reason with herself. But it had been years since any man had stirred her with a prickle of sexual interest. So why was this one stirring up cold ashes?

"That's why I do it," he told her.

Mercedes was studying his face, trying to read beneath the surface of his words when Lex suddenly called to her from across the lawn.

"Hey, Mercedes, come here! A long lost stranger has arrived!"

Glancing over her shoulder, she saw Lex standing with an old classmate of hers. Vernon Sweeney, the nerd of St. Mary's High School. He was sweet and not nearly as exciting as the man standing in front of her. But he was safe. And right now safe was far easier to handle.

Turning back to Gabe, she swiftly explained, "An old friend calls. Will you excuse me?"

His stoic expression didn't falter. "Certainly, Ms. Saddler."

For the next hour, Mercedes mingled, talked, laughed and danced with the endless guests that spilled across the two hundred feet of lawn separating the big house from the old bunkhouse.

She'd been home for just a little over a week and truthfully hadn't had time to get her feet firmly planted back on Sandbur soil when her mother had started planning tonight's event. Mercedes hadn't really been up to this much socializing so soon. She would have preferred to get back in the groove of civilian life before being tossed into a crowd. But this homecoming was important to her mother and she'd not wanted to hurt her feelings for any reason. And these were her friends, she reminded herself. All of them except Gabe Trevino.

In spite of the evening's distractions of dancing, eating and reacquainting herself with old friends, she'd not been able to get the dark horseman off her mind. Which was really very foolish of her. They'd not exchanged more than a handful of sentences, and the few words he'd directed at her had been polite—nothing out of line. Yet she thought there had been an underlying condescension in his attitude, as though he found her boring or, even worse, a spoiled brat. She continued to bristle at the idea as her brother whirled her around the dance floor.

"Still as light on your feet as ever," Lex said with a grin. "Guess all those ballet lessons you took as a child are still paying off."

She laughed. "Poor Mother. I don't think I ever quit fighting her about those."

"You wanted to wear chaps instead of a frilly tutu."

Mercedes sighed. It seemed so long ago since she'd been that innocent age. If only her life had remained that simple and sheltered. "I was a tomboy. She wanted me to be more refined, like Nicci. So did Daddy."

"Nah. Dad loved you any way you wanted to be," he said.

She couldn't help but notice a tiny shadow crossing her brother's handsome face. He still missed their father desperately. Mercedes missed him, too. She'd give anything to have him here with them. But back in 1996, Paul Saddler had died in what the police had called a boating accident. To this day, Lex didn't like to discuss the tragedy or say one way or the other what he believed happened that fateful day on the Gulf. All Mercedes knew was that her father was gone and their lives were far lesser because of it.

"Enjoying yourself, sis?"

She smiled up at him. "Certainly. It's a very nice party. Mother has outdone herself. And Cook still has her special touch, doesn't she? The brisket melted in my mouth."

"Bet you didn't have anything like that over on Diego Garcia."

No. The military air base located on the tiny island in the Indian Ocean didn't cater to parties or home-cooked Texas meals. She'd spent the last two years of her eight-year stint in the Air Force on the isolated island and had to admit that she'd forgotten just what a spoiled, luxurious life she'd once had here on the Sandbur.

"We had turkey and pecan pie on Thanksgiving," she said,

then laughed. "'Course, it had to be flown in—just like everything else."

Lex's smile was full of affection. "We've missed you, honey. Everyone is so glad to have you back home. We're all going to give you hell if you try to leave again. Just keep that in mind if you get the urge to travel."

Her brother's words made her feel wanted, yet at the same time uncomfortable. He and the rest of the family had simply taken it for granted that she was home to stay. But Mercedes wasn't at all sure that her life was meant to be spent on the ranch. Not when old memories and past mistakes continued to haunt her at every turn.

She was trying to push the unsettling issue of her future out of her mind when her gaze slipped past Lex's shoulder to another couple circling the dance floor. So far this evening, she'd not spotted the horse trainer taking a turn to the music. She'd already decided the man wasn't into dancing, but it looked as if she was wrong.

Alice Woodson, an old classmate of Mercedes's, was snuggled up to him, looking as though she was enjoying every second of being in his arms. She would, Mercedes thought with a measure of sarcasm. The woman was man-crazy and had been since junior high.

"Yoo-hoo, sis! The song is over. Want to go another round?"

Realizing the music and her brother's feet had both stopped, Mercedes looked up at him and hoped her wandering thoughts didn't show. "I think I'll sit this one out, Lex. I'm ready to get something to drink."

Looping his arm around her waist, Lex ushered Mercedes off the dance floor. As the two of them walked to the nearest galvanized tub of iced drinks, Mercedes couldn't help but ask, "Do you know why Mother invited Alice?"

Lex frowned. "She's one of your old classmates, isn't she?"

"Yes. But I never cared for her," Mercedes muttered. "Although it seems that someone around here does."

Lex followed Mercedes's gaze as she watched Gabe escort Alice off the dance floor and over to a nearby table.

"Gabe and Alice?" Lex laughed. "He's just being gentlemanly. I don't think Gabe is much into women."

Mercedes frowned as she reached down and plucked a diet soda from among the assortment of drinks. "What do you mean?"

Lex shrugged as though he didn't much want to elaborate, which only made Mercedes even more curious.

Lex finally said, "I think he's had a bad experience and doesn't care to repeat it."

Mercedes could certainly understand that. She'd spent the past eight years dodging men, telling herself that being alone was much better than having her heart ripped out, her trust shattered again.

Popping open the can, she took a sip as she covertly studied the horseman out of the corner of her eye. He was a tall devil, shaped like a wedge with strong broad shoulders and narrow hips. His jeans and Western shirt were probably pieces of clothing that he wore to work every day. Yet he wore the casual garments with so much class that he made all the other men seem ridiculously overdressed.

Mercedes's lips pressed together as she watched Alice place a hand on Gabe's arm. "Then he'd better stay away from Alice. She'll try to devour him."

Lex chuckled. "If you're so worried about the man, why don't you go to the rescue and ask him for a dance?"

Mercedes stared in thoughtful surprise at her brother. Back in high school, she'd been bold enough to ask a guy for a dance, or even a date. But once she'd grown older, once she'd loved and lost, her courage with men had faltered. Then later, when she'd learned the hard way that trusting a man was equal to rolling a dice, her desire to be close to one in any circumstance had dwindled down to nothing.

"Me?" she asked. "No. I'm not the type to ask a man to do anything."

"Getting a little haughty, are we?"

Haughty? If she told her brother how insecure she really felt, he'd be shocked. But she didn't want him to know that his once fearless sister had changed to a cautious soul, that she saw men as things that could hurt her rather than give her pleasure and companionship. "No," she said curtly. "More like getting smart."

With a roll of his eyes, Lex shook his head at her. "Coward."

Why was it that her brother had always known exactly how to push her buttons? He could have said anything else and it would have rolled off her back. But being home on the ranch reminded her that being a Saddler meant facing a challenge head on. Mercedes wanted her brother to see she was still worthy of the family name.

With a toss of her head, she gave Lex a cunning smile and then started off in Gabriel Trevino's direction. After all, the worst the man could do was turn her down. And even if he did, it was only a little dance. She wouldn't let it bother her.

Alice saw her coming first and Mercedes watched a plastic smile form on the other woman's face.

"Mercedes, have I told you tonight how fabulous you look?" Alice asked as Mercedes edged up to the table where the pair were sitting in folding metal chairs. "The Air Force must be getting lax, 'cause you look as if you've spent the past month in a spa. 'Course, it wasn't as if you were toting a gun through the jungle or anything."

Mercedes merely looked at the woman, and Alice, sensing she'd just chewed on her own foot, began to giggle nervously.

"It's great to see you, Alice. I'm glad you could make it tonight," Mercedes said politely, then turned a questioning gaze on Gabe. "Would you care to dance with me, Mr. Trevino? When the band starts playing Bob Wills, I can't keep my feet still and Lex is all tuckered out."

"Yeah, Lex looks plumb beat," Alice said mockingly.

Ignoring the other woman's jab, Mercedes watched Gabe's gray eyes flicker with surprise, but then slowly he rose to his feet and reached for her arm.

He said, "Excuse me," to Alice, and the woman made some sort of reply, but Mercedes didn't hear it. Her ears were roaring with her own heartbeat as the two of them walked toward the elevated dance floor.

"What was that all about?" he asked once they were a few steps away from Alice. "You have a grudge against that woman?"

"Not really. I just thought you ought to know she's a man-eater. She's already been through two husbands and she hasn't celebrated her thirtieth birthday yet."

To her surprise, he chuckled.

"Do I look like a man who can't take care of himself?"

He looked like a man who could take care of anything. But she'd only just met the man; she was hardly ready to give him a gushing compliment.

"I don't know. Can you?"

"I've survived thirty-five years," he said curtly. "I'm doing okay."

By the time they reached the dance floor, the western swing number had finished and the lead singer began to sing a slow ballad about lost love. It wasn't the sort of dance she'd intended to have with Gabe Trevino, but there wasn't much she could do about it now except step into his arms and move to the music.

"Why did you ask me to dance?" he asked bluntly as his hand settled at the back of her waist.

His arms were rock-hard and though she tried to keep space between the front of her body and his, her breasts brushed against his chest and her thigh slid between his. In spite of their slow pace, she felt a desperate need for oxygen as her body began to hum with excitement.

"Actually, Lex challenged me to ask you," she said honestly. "You see, I was worried about you and Alice. He thought I ought to rescue you. So did I."

"I don't know whether to feel flattered or insulted."

And she didn't know why, after several years of celibacy, this stranger had woken her sleeping libido. "I wouldn't bother with either," she said as casually as she could. "It's just a dance."

Even though her head was turned to one side, she knew he was looking down at her. She could feel his gaze examining the side of her face, then dropping to the V neckline of her dress. At the same time, the hand at the back of her waist slid upward until his fingers splayed against her bare back.

From somewhere deep inside her, a flame unexpectedly flickered, then burst into an all-out inferno. Dismayed that she was reacting to him so strongly, she could only thank God that it was dark and he couldn't see the droplets of sweat collecting on her upper lip.

"I thought maybe you were just feeling generous," he said close to her ear. "Wanting to give the hired help a dance with royalty."

Easing her head back, she glowered at him. "Look, just so you know, I don't think of myself as a princess or you as hired help. You have a chip on your shoulder or something?"

Gabe had never felt sorry for himself or his position in life. He was proud of who and what he was. Maybe he needed to make that clear to her. "I just don't need for you to feel sorry for me, Ms. Saddler. I like myself."

She surprised him by laughing. Not just one short sound of amusement, but a long laugh filled with joy. Yet instead of feeling annoyed with her, the infectious sound put a grin on his face.

"Please, call me Mercedes. And just to set your mind at ease, Gabe, you're the last person I would think needs sympathy."

She felt like a dream in his arms, he thought. A soft warm dream where one pleasure seeped into another and every spot he touched thrilled him just that much more.

He struggled to control himself. Hell, just because it had been a long time since he'd had a woman didn't mean this one was supposed to turn him into a randy buck, he thought with self-disgust. So what if she was as sexy as sin? That didn't mean he needed her any closer than she already was. No, sir, he'd already learned the hard way the price he'd have to pay for a woman like her.

"I heard Alice say something about the Air Force. Is that why you've been away from the ranch? Because you were in the Air Force?"

"Eight years," she answered. "My job was intelligence gathering."

It just didn't fit, Gabe pondered. A woman like her didn't need to work, much less go into the strict, disciplined life of the military. He had to admit that he admired her ambition. Even more, he had to admit that he wanted to know what was really behind those deep blue eyes staring back at him.

"What made you decide to enter the military?"

One of her shoulders lifted and fell with nonchalance, but he noticed that her gaze deliberately swung away from his.

"You and I are more alike than you think, Gabe. I like a challenge, too."

He didn't figure she was giving him the complete reason. But then he hadn't expected her to spill her life's story through one slow dance.

"What about you?" she asked. "How did you come to be here on the Sandbur?"

"I met Cordero at a horse seminar over in Louisiana. He liked my work and asked me if I'd be interested in settling here."

"And you were," she stated the obvious.

"Here I am."

She seemed on the verge of asking him more when the song suddenly ended.

"Want to go another round?" he asked.

She smiled. "I really shouldn't ignore the other guests who've come to see me tonight."

"Then thank you very much for the dance." He lifted the back of her hand to his lips and pressed a kiss on the soft skin.

Wide-eyed, she asked, "Did you give one of those to Alice, too?"

A faint grin curved the corner of his mouth. "No. She didn't dance nearly as well as you."

She studied him for several long, awkward moments and then smiled impishly. "Oh. Well, I won't wipe it off, then," she said brightly. Before he could make any sort of reply, she pulled out of his embrace and hurried off the dance floor.

Gabe stared after her and wondered why he felt as though he'd just taken a hard tumble from the saddle.

## Chapter Two

Once the party finally ended, Mercedes didn't get into bed until the wee hours of the morning. Though she was exhausted, her sleep ended abruptly when she woke up long before daylight, her body drenched in sweat, her senses disoriented.

Swinging her legs over the side of the bed, she pressed a hand to her damp face.

*You're okay, Mercedes. You're in your old bedroom on the Sandbur. The bedroom where you played as a child, had sleepovers with friends.*

Dropping her hand from her bleary eyes, she gazed around at the shadows shrouding the walls and furniture while she waited for the axis of her brain to spin in the right direction.

She'd been dreaming, she realized, but not of something pleasant or peaceful. The dream had involved a man and a horse inside a corral. She'd been watching from the fence, calling out to him, trying to warn him that he was about to be hurt. The horse had charged, knocked the man down, then reared and viciously brought his front hoofs down on the man's back.

*Gabe!* She'd been dreaming about Gabe Trevino. The realization stunned her almost as much as the vivid dream had shocked her senses. She'd not gone to bed thinking of the man much. Well, maybe that tiny kiss on the back of her hand *had* fluttered through her thoughts right before she'd gone to sleep, she corrected herself. But her mind certainly hadn't been consumed by the man.

With a rough sigh, she rose from the bed and stumbled into the bathroom. She might as well shower and start the day, because there was no way she could go back to sleep now.

A few minutes later, Mercedes, dressed in jeans, boots and a cool summer shirt, walked through the quiet house. In the kitchen, she realized that she'd even beaten Cook out of bed. The room was still dark.

For a brief moment, she considered making a pot of coffee, then decided she'd wait until the rest of the family was up to enjoy it with her.

Instead, she let herself out of the house through a back exit and made her way through the dark early morning to the horse barn. Across the way, she could see a faint light glowing in the bunkhouse. The wranglers would be stirring soon, catching their mounts and saddling them up for the day's work ahead.

Mourning doves were cooing and mockingbirds were beginning to flitter to life among the live oaks. There was a peaceful beauty to the ranch that Mercedes had always loved. Even when the ranch yard bustled with life, it was a poetry of sights and sounds. The hammer of the farrier, the bawl of a calf, the nicker of a horse, the sun coming up and the moon going down.

From generation to generation and year after year, her family had worked and carved this ranch from prickly pear patches and endless stretches of mesquite trees. As for Mercedes, she'd been born here in her parents' bedroom.

Yes, she'd been rooted here. But eight long years ago, she'd pulled up those roots and run as fast and hard as she could. Now she wondered if she'd made a mistake by coming back, trying to make this her home once again, trying to pretend that she could fall back into the life she'd led before her college life and John's big deception, before her stint at Peterson AFB and the humiliating mistake she carried from there.

Trying to shake away the nagging questions, she walked on to the barn and climbed up on a board fence that corralled a small herd of yearling horses. From a lofty seat on the top rail, she watched the colts and fillies play in the cool morning air until she heard a footfall behind her.

Glancing over her shoulder, she was more than surprised to see the man of her disturbing dream propping his shoulder against the board fence. He was dressed in a dark blue denim shirt with pearl snaps, the standard fare that cowboys had worn for decades. Funny how the shirt looked tailored just for him. Some men tried to play the part, while others were naturals. She realized that Gabe was one of those naturals, the epitome of all things Western right down to the square toes of his brown cowboy boots.

"You're up very early," he remarked.

"So are you. Today is Saturday," she pointed out. "Don't tell me that you start your workday this early on a Saturday."

Even though he had no way of knowing that she'd dreamed about him, the fact that he'd shouldered his way into her subconscious thoughts was enough to put a sting of embarrassment on her cheeks.

He jerked his head toward the pen full of horses. "They don't know it's a weekend."

He was right. Nothing stopped on the ranch. At the least, livestock had to be fed and cared for every day of the week.

She drew in a long breath and let it out as she guided her gaze back to the pen of horses. "Are all of these broken to the halter?" she asked.

"Yes."

"What are you doing with them now?"

"Getting them used to blankets and saddles on their backs. When they get closer to two, I'll put someone lightweight like you on them. Ever ride a green horse?"

Even though he was standing on the ground and a good foot away from her, his presence was a huge thing, crowding toward her, making her completely aware of her femininity.

She answered, "I've ridden a few outlaws before. But as for green horses, only once. Daddy forbade us to climb on anything that wasn't completely broken to ride, but I didn't always do what I was told."

"Imagine that."

Even though she didn't glance at him, she could hear a smile in his voice, and the sound warmed her, drew her to him.

"Yeah. I got bucked off and broke my arm. I missed the whole softball season at school that year. I learned about green horses the hard way."

Apparently she'd always been an outdoors person, Gabe thought. The notion surprised him, although it shouldn't have. She'd been in the military, after all. She'd had to go through rigorous physical preparation to graduate basic training. Still, she seemed so womanly, so soft, that he couldn't imagine her in camouflaged fatigues or wearing a pair of spurs and chaps.

"Don't feel badly, we've all been dumped," he told her.

She remained quiet and after a few moments, Gabe glanced up to see her wiping her hands down her thighs as she rose from her seat on the fence. She was wearing a blue and white patterned shirt with short sleeves. A white scarf was twisted and tied around her thick hair. Once she was standing on the ground, he could see her face was void of makeup, yet it held as much color and beauty as the sun breaking over the treetops.

Smiling faintly, she said, "I'd better get back to the house. I haven't had any coffee yet, or breakfast."

"I can't do anything about the breakfast, but I've just made a pot of fresh coffee. Would you care to join me for a cup?"

She glanced questioningly around her. "Here?"

He jerked his head toward the barn. "I've got an office inside the barn."

Surprise arched her brows. "I thought Cordero's office was over by the cattle barn."

"It's still there. But I like it here—keeps me closer to the foaling mares. And your mother kindly supplied me with a few things to make it comfortable."

She gestured toward the building situated several yards behind him. "I'd like to see this new office of yours," she agreed. "And I'd especially like the coffee."

Built when the Sandbur had first become a full-fledged ranch in 1900, the barn was one of the few original structures that had weathered more than a century of the extreme climate of South Texas. Because the building was made of heavy lumber, it stayed cooler in the summer and warmer in the winter than some of the newer barns that were built from corrugated iron. It had always been one of Mercedes's favorite spots on the ranch.

As the two of them stepped inside the cavernous building, Gabe took Mercedes by the arm and guided her down a long, wide alleyway to a closed door. Gabe opened it and gestured for her to enter.

The moment she stepped into the room, she was immediately impressed with the large teacher's desk and office chair, the computer, fax and copier, telephone, refrigerator and small cooking element. "Why, this used to be a tack room," she said with amazement. "How did you make such a transformation?"

"Me and some of the hands partitioned off part of the feed room and moved all the riding equipment in there." He gestured for her to take a seat on the long couch running against one wood-paneled wall. "Sit down. You might recognize that couch. It came from the den in the big house. Your mother said she needed a new one anyway. I think she was just being generous. During foaling season, I need a place to stretch out from time to time."

While she made herself comfortable on the couch, Gabe poured coffee into two foam cups.

"Cream or sugar? Or both?" he asked.

"Cream. Just a splash. But I can do it."

She started to rise from her seat, but he motioned her back down. "I can manage."

Back at the couch, Gabe handed her the steaming coffee and then took a seat on the cushion next to her. Other than Geraldine Saddler, no woman had set foot in his private domain until now. It seemed strange and even more distracting for Mercedes to be sitting only inches away from him.

"Mmm. Thank you," she murmured as she lifted the steaming drink to her lips.

As he sipped from his own cup, he realized he shouldn't have invited her in here. In fact, he shouldn't have danced with her last night. Because even now he was assaulted with the memories of her curvy body brushing temptingly against his, the scent of her skin, the softness of her sigh as it skittered against the side of his neck. He couldn't remember a time that any woman had left such an indelible impression on him, and that could only mean trouble. Mercedes was rich, strong and independent—just like the woman who'd married him, then smashed him into useless pieces.

"So you're home now," he said. "What do you plan to do with your time?"

She stared into her cup rather than at him. "I—I'm not sure yet. For starters, I'm going to give myself a few days to adjust to civilian life."

She could afford to do that, Gabe thought. In fact, she could afford to do anything she wanted to do. He couldn't imagine having *that* much financial security. Sherleen had been rich, before and after they'd married. Not nearly as rich as Mercedes or her family, but wealthy enough. As her husband, Gabe had never considered his wife's money as his, too. In fact, he'd never wanted it and had done his best to pay his own way throughout their short years together. A man of any stock didn't want to be labeled as being kept by his wife. And to Gabe, riches weren't measured by the balance in a bank account. Unfortunately, his ex-wife had thought differently. Now he found himself attracted to another rich woman. What the hell was the matter with him, anyway? He'd learned the hard way that he and wealthy women didn't mix.

He said, "I guess that was a stupid question on my part, anyway."

Her eyes were full of questions as they roamed his face and Gabe realized he needed to be more careful or his personal feelings would show.

"Why do you say that?"

What the hell, he thought. He wasn't going to tiptoe around

this woman as though she were royalty. "Nothing. Just that—well, it's not like you have to go out and find a job."

Disgust turned the corners of her lips downward as she rose from her seat to amble around the tiny room. "I can't read your mind, Gabe. So I don't have any idea what sort of impressions you have about me. But I can assure you that I don't plan to sit on my hands."

"I wouldn't think so," he drawled with a bit of sarcasm. "It might flatten them."

She shot him a droll look and then chuckled. "Smart mouth. I'll bet as a teenager you gave your mother fits."

A dark cloud suddenly shadowed his thoughts. Though he reminded himself that this woman was teasing, that she couldn't know about Jenna Trevino's death, it still hurt to think of growing up without his mother and the horrible way she'd left this world.

"No. I didn't give her fits," he said curtly. "She was in her grave."

Mercedes couldn't have felt more awful. She wanted to walk behind the desk and crawl inside the knee hole, but hiding would hardly help her now. "Oh, boy, I messed up there, didn't I?" she murmured more to herself than to him. Glancing regretfully at the man, she tried again, "Gabe, I— You're a young man. I just assumed that your mother was still alive. Forgive me."

She watched him draw in a long breath, then release it, and from the strained expression on his face, she got the notion that he felt more awkward than even she did.

"Forget it, Mercedes. You didn't know."

Afraid she'd worsen her foot-in-mouth disease with any sort of reply, she waited for him to say more, anything that would explain how his mother died. But after several more clumsy moments passed in silence, she decided it best to change the subject completely.

Resting a hip on the corner of the desk, she said, "So. What do you use the computer for? Keeping track of sales?"

"Yes. And I also keep a file for every horse on the Sandbur. It's a big help in keeping track of their breeding, farrier visits, vaccinations, injuries, progress in their training. You get the picture."

Mercedes was very impressed. Her cousin Cordero was a good horse trainer, but he'd never been that meticulous about keeping data. "You sound like a doctor keeping updates on his patients' charts."

"Exactly. I'll show you."

Leaving the couch, he walked past her and went to stand behind the desk. Mercedes swiveled around to see him switching on the computer. While the machine whirred to life, she used the time to study him from beneath a pair of lowered lashes.

Apparently he'd not taken the time to shave this morning. A black stubble of beard covered his jaws, upper lip and chin. His hair, what she could see of it beneath the brim of his hat, curled damply against the back of his neck, as though it hadn't been long since he'd stepped out of the shower. The scent of soap and musk and man all swirled together and drifted across the small space between them.

Stirred in spite of herself, she looked away and made a steeple of her hands. For the past eight years, she'd worked around men on a daily basis. Some of them had been good-looking, even sexy. A few had become buddies. And one— Well, she'd thought Drew was a very special friend until he'd proved not to be a friend at all. But even before his betrayal, she'd never found his flirtatious smile and rumbling laugh this distracting. He'd never had her thinking of hot nights, sweaty sheets or even a slow, wet kiss the way this man was doing now.

Mercedes believed the sexual side of her had died along with her dreams of finding love. Yet for some reason she couldn't understand, Gabe Trevino seemed to be shaking her back to life.

"Okay," he said, breaking into her thoughts. "Here's a chart on He's A Peppy Charge. Take a look."

Attempting to shake away the sensual fog settling over her, Mercedes placed her coffee mug on the desk then walked around to stand next to him. With every ounce of strength in her, she forced herself to focus on the monitor screen rather than him.

"Everything is here," she observed. "His birthday, family tree, color and markings, vet visits, blood tests." She scanned the data until she reached Gabe's personal comments and then she read aloud, "Deceptive charmer. Tries to buck if not completely warmed up. Great speed and athleticism. Needs experienced cowboy on his back."

A provocative smile curved her lips as she turned her head to look at him. "Does that mean you?"

The moment she saw his eyes narrow, Mercedes knew she'd struck a nerve and nudged him over the invisible line that had been acting as a polite barrier between them.

As he moved closer, she sucked in a bracing breath.

"Just what are you doing here, anyway, Ms. Saddler?"

Gabe had never intended to let this woman provoke him. From the moment he'd spotted her on the fence, he'd planned to appear cool and collected, even if his insides felt like a boiler on the verge of exploding. But now the teasing glint in her sexy blue eyes made him forget all about his earlier determination. Now his focus refused to go beyond the moist pout of her lips, the idea of how she would taste and feel.

"Uh—what do you mean?" she asked hoarsely.

Before Gabe could stop himself, he wrapped his hand around her forearm and tugged her against him. As her breast flattened against his chest, he could feel her heart flutter, and his own begin to pound.

"I mean, here," he clipped out. "At the horse barn. Where you knew you would find me."

Gabe hated the way her soft curves aroused him, yet at the same time, he couldn't deny the excitement rushing through his veins.

Scowling at him, she said, "I walked down to the horse pen because it's a nice, cool morning and I wanted to get out of the house. This is the last place I thought you would be."

Her lame excuse filled his snort with a mix of humor and sarcasm. "Really? This is where I work. Where did you think I'd be?"

"In bed. Where everyone else is right now!"

Her nostrils flared like a filly being circled by a stallion, and Gabe felt a hot, feral flame flicker deep inside him.

"Everyone is in bed—but you and me," he pointed out lowly.

Her tongue darted out to moisten her lips and it was all Gabe could do to keep from closing the last bit of space between their faces. "If you think—"

"I think a whole lot of things," he bluntly interrupted, "but I know we're both thinking about this."

Mercedes wasn't sure if he tugged her forward or if she simply wilted against him, but the next thing she knew his mouth was hot and heavy on hers, his arms were wrapped around her shoulders, anchoring her upper body against his.

The intimate connection was such a shock to Mercedes's senses that the thought of resisting didn't have time to enter her mind. And then as his lips began to search and plunder her mouth, she realized that she didn't want to resist. She didn't want to do anything but stand in the circle of his arms and drink in the heady taste of him.

Somewhere outside, she heard a rooster crow, a horse snort, another squeal. Inside the room a clock was *tick, tick, ticking*. Or was that the sound of her heart beating in her ears? She couldn't tell anymore. Her senses were beginning to melt into a useless puddle.

A keening moan gurgled in the back of her throat as her hands searched for some sort of support. It came in the way of his hard shoulders, and her fingers were about to latch over them when he suddenly jerked back from her.

The abrupt separation of their bodies tilted Mercedes's footing and left her snatching a steadying hold on the edge of the desk. As she stared at him in stunned fascination, she felt her lips burning, her lungs dragging in long ragged breaths.

After several hard swallows, she finally managed to ask, "What—what was that all about?"

His jaw hardened as his gray gaze swept over her flushed face. "To let you know that I don't play games, Mercedes. Not with you. Not with any woman. Try it again and I promise you—you'll get burned."

Straightening her shoulders, she lifted her chin. "Pompous ass," she snarled at him. "Do you think every woman that gets within speaking distance of you wants to crawl into your bed?"

Without warning, his hand shot out and cuffed around her upper arm. Mercedes glanced down at his fingers biting into her flesh and then she saw them—tough welts of jagged scars on top of his wrist and disappearing beneath the cuff of his shirt.

Somewhere, somehow he'd been terribly injured. The visual evidence, even the mere thought, shocked Mercedes almost as much as his kiss had, and for long moments she couldn't tear her eyes away from his brown skin.

"Gabe, your—"

Before she could say more, he jerked his hand away and quickly stepped back from her.

"Get out of here, Mercedes," he gritted. "Go find some other man to amuse you."

She couldn't believe that only seconds before sympathy for the man had swept through her. Right now, she'd love to slap his jaw.

"In case you've forgotten, the Sandbur is my home. I'm not going to tiptoe around you as though you're something special. If I want to come here to the horse barn or anywhere else on the ranch where you just happened to be, I will! And if you don't like it, you can just—go!"

Not about to wait for any sort of reply from the man, Mercedes stomped out of the little office and marched down the alleyway of the barn. By now, sunlight was slanting through the door of the cavernous building, shedding light on the stalls lined against both walls. Several horses were sticking their heads over gates, watching her movements. Under normal circumstances, she would have stopped and greeted every animal. As it was, her lips were on fire, her eyes stinging with tears, and she couldn't get out of the barn fast enough.

Back in the tiny office, Gabe switched off the computer and slumped into the desk chair, then immediately jumped back up and grabbed his coffee cup. As he splashed more hot liquid over the portion that had cooled, he muttered several choice curse words at himself. He didn't know what in hell had come over him or possessed him to grab the woman, much less kiss her.

She'd done nothing more than tease him. And she'd done it gently, at that. Nothing she'd said or done had warranted his behavior. Even if she had come down to the barn purposely to see him, even if she *was* using him to amuse herself, that didn't mean he should have taken the bait. He liked to think he was older and wiser than to let his head be turned by a pretty face.

But the moment she'd stood next to him, her face only inches away, her scent drifting over him, tantalizing every cell in his body, his common sense had crawled out the door. Now just the memory of her lips beneath his, the feel of her hands moving against his chest was enough to leave him hard and frustrated.

*So what are you going to do now, Gabe?*

Remind himself that he was nothing more than a hired hand and get to work.

## Chapter Three

Later that morning, Mercedes was in her bedroom, trying to motivate herself to finish unpacking the boxes that were stacked in one corner. So far, she'd done little more than hang a few garments in the armoire.

What was she really doing here on the ranch, anyway? she asked herself for the umpteenth time. Was she really home to stay, or was she simply using the ranch as a launching pad to some other job at some other place?

Sighing wistfully, she dropped the slinky blouse back to the open box lying upon the bed and walked over to a huge arched window. Since her upstairs bedroom was on the west end of the house, the window was partially shaded by the enormous limbs of a live oak, yet through the break in the leaves she could see a part of the ranch yard and a small portion of the horse barn. Just looking at the old barn and recalling her encounter with Gabe Trevino was enough to make her blush.

Unwittingly, her fingertips lifted to her lips. She'd never been kissed like that before, as though she were a piece of meat and he a starving animal. It was embarrassing to think how much the kiss had excited her, had shaken the very core of her womanhood.

She'd thought John had been an adept lover. She'd believed that she would never meet another man whose touch would sweep her senses into such a mushy state of bliss. But Gabe had done that and more. Those few moments in his arms had left her feeling like a hungry tigress. She'd wanted to tear at his clothes and her own. She'd wanted to surrender to him completely. It was frightening to think how he'd woken her sleeping sexuality and turned it into a sizzling libido.

"Darling, you haven't even gotten started with these boxes. Would you like for Alida to come up and help you?"

At the sound of her mother's voice, Mercedes turned away from the window to see that Geraldine had walked into the room. Concern was on her face as her gaze flicked from her daughter to the still packed boxes.

"Mother, I didn't have a maid in the Air Force. I hardly need one now."

Geraldine scowled. "No need to get huffy. I was just offering. Or would you rather I help you?"

"No. I can manage," she insisted. Spotting the faint look of hurt on her mother's face, she crossed the space between them and pecked a kiss on her smooth cheek. "I don't mean to sound sharp, Mother. I'm tired, that's all. This past week has been a little hectic. I don't think I've caught up from the jet lag yet."

Mercedes didn't go on to say that having a maid in the house made her feel guilty and overly pampered, especially after some of the pitiful sights she'd endured while on rescue missions in America and abroad. Floods, fires, earthquakes. The U.S. military stepped in to help when natural catastrophes shredded people's lives and left them homeless and frightened. In those cases, having necessities was the difference between living or dying. The word *maid* didn't exist in that reality.

Geraldine turned a sympathetic smile on her daughter. "And the party last night went on forever," she conceded. "I guess I should have waited to throw it. But everyone has been so excited about you coming home. I didn't want to wait."

Nodding that she understood, Mercedes went over to the queen-size bed and sat on the edge of the mattress. "I'm glad you didn't wait. I enjoyed seeing everyone again."

Geraldine walked over to a nearby armchair and sank into it. As she crossed her long legs, Mercedes couldn't help thinking that her mother had hardly aged the past eight years. She was quite slim and shapely for a woman of sixty-four. Her complexion was tanned and smooth, while her silver hair sparkled with life. This past year, she'd started to date again, a widowed Texas senator. Mercedes admired her courage and was especially glad that she'd never given up on life after her husband had died.

*The way you've given up on men?* Maybe she had given up on men, she told herself, but she had good reason—they weren't to be trusted.

"Darling, we've not done anything to this room since you left for the Air Force," Geraldine commented as she looked around the room. "Maybe you'd like a change. New paint? Drapes? Furniture?"

The walls of the room were a soft, textured pink and the furniture was antique heavy oak that had been here since her grandparents' heyday. She didn't want to change a thing about the room. It was *herself* that Mercedes needed to change. But she didn't have a clue how to start. How did a person forget pain and betrayal? How could she ever have a family of her own if she couldn't trust a man to take out the garbage on time, much less take care of her heart?

Mercedes's gaze joined her mother's as it traveled around the walls that were crowded with photos and paintings, then down to the Spanish tile scattered with thick looped throw rugs. "There's nothing wrong with this room, Mother. I don't want it changed."

Seeming not to hear her, Geraldine went on, "Well, since Nicci's moved out, you could take over her room if you like it better."

Now that Nicci had married Ridge and given birth to a new daughter, Sara Rose, her sister's bedroom was empty. As empty as Mercedes's heart.

"No," Mercedes said flatly. "I'm happy here."

Geraldine's lips pursed together. "You hardly look as if you're happy, Mercedes. And I don't mean to push you, but frankly, I'm worried about you, honey. I thought—" She paused and shook her head with frustration. "Well, let's just say that I hoped coming home would make you feel differently about things."

Mercedes plucked at the knobby bedspread. "What things?"

"Well, dammit, I'm not going to beat around the bush with you. I never have, so I don't guess I should start now. I'm talking about that bastard—John. And don't tell me that you're still not moping about him. I would have thought that after eight years, you would have gotten the man out of your system. But no, I still catch you staring off into space with that my-world-has-ended look. Frankly, Mercedes, I'm sick of seeing it."

Geraldine's angry words snapped Mercedes's head up.

"That's not true! I'm not moping about John Layton. Good Lord, Mother, it's like you just said, that was more than eight years ago!"

"But you haven't forgotten."

How could she forget the most humiliating, heartbreaking experience of her life? John had been her history professor at the University of Texas. He'd been a quiet, serious man, highly intellectual and handsome to boot. When he'd first shown a romantic interest in Mercedes, she'd been completely bowled over by his charm. Later, as their relationship had progressed into a full-blown affair, she'd truly believed that he loved her and wanted to marry her. She'd thought that the two of them together could conquer the world. God, she'd looked at him and the world through rose-colored glasses.

Sighing, she tried to explain. "Look, Mother, I believed John was the love of my life. I thought he was going to be my husband. The father of my children!"

"Instead, you learned in an offhanded way that he already had a wife with a child on the way. Believe me, Mercedes, that would have been enough to wipe all memories of love or anything else from my mind. Apparently, you're different from me. I guess I'm just too hard-hearted to let some no-account, playboy college professor ruin my life."

It was just like her mother to lay the whole affair out in such blunt terms. She didn't play favorites with her children. She treated them all with the same tough love.

"I don't still care for the man, if that's what you're thinking, Mother. In fact, I couldn't care less what has happened to him. It's just that the whole thing with John made me see how easy it is to be duped by a man. I'm not sure that I'll ever be able to trust another one."

Mercedes didn't go on to explain to her mother that John's deception was only a part of her reluctance to enter another relationship with a man. Three years ago, she'd been terribly betrayed by Airman Drew Downy. Because of him, her security status had been lowered and she'd been reprimanded severely for her lapse in judgment. It had taken months of hard work for her to regain the trust of her superior officers. All because she'd trusted a man. Because she'd believed he was a good friend and had truly cared for her. But instead of being loyal, Drew had blown the whistle on her for sharing classified secrets that *he* had prompted her to disclose. The memory still made her cringe with humiliation and hurt.

Even though Drew hadn't been her lover, Mercedes had believed their relationship might grow and blossom into something lasting. When she finally figured out that he was only using her to show himself in a positive light, she'd been crushed and shocked that she'd once again so misjudged a man. After that, she'd gone numb and so guarded that she was reluctant to even share the time of day with a male counterpart in a social context.

"God help you," Geraldine murmured.

Trying to swallow away the ball of bitterness in her throat, Mercedes thrust a hand through her thick hair. "Mother, I have other things on my mind. And they hardly revolve around finding a man."

Looking extremely disgusted now, Geraldine tapped her fingers against the arm of the chair. "Okay. So you want to put sex and love and marriage last on your to-do list. What's first?"

Mercedes quickly glanced away from her mother as this morning's encounter with Gabe danced through her thoughts. Sex had hardly been the last thing on her mind when he'd planted that sizzling lock on her lips. But pure sex was all it had been, she told herself. And she wasn't planning on letting it happen again. Not if she could help it.

Trying to shake the memory away, she said firmly, "I want to be productive, Mother. Useful. I want to feel as though I'm where I'm supposed to be."

Clearly concerned with her daughter's attitude, Geraldine left the chair and came to stand in front of Mercedes. "Honey, I know with your training in intelligence you could easily get a job most anywhere you wanted. You'd be making good money—not that you need it, but you'd have it to fall back on if, God forbid, the ranch ever slid into a losing hole. But I'm not all that sure that throwing yourself into a government job is what you really need at this time in your life."

Not bothering to hide her unsettled thoughts, Mercedes held her palms up in a helpless gesture. "I'm not sure it's what I need, either. But what am I supposed to do, Mother? I'm not the idle type. And I can't simply chase cows from morning 'til night."

And she sure as heck wasn't going to work with the horses and face Gabe Trevino every day, Mercedes thought. Her peace of mind would be torn to shreds.

"There's more to do around here than chase cows! Ask your brother. Ask your cousin Matt. They work themselves to the ground every day to keep this place in the black. Maybe it's time someone else in the family offered to step up to the plate and do their part!"

Mercedes was cut to the quick by her mother's retort, and she couldn't utter one word in reply. Instead, she rose from the bed and brushed past Geraldine. At one end of the room, rows of wide wooden shelves held souvenirs and mementos from her past. A 4-H trophy for best heifer at the state fair.

Another for horsemanship. A rhinestone tiara from when she'd won Miss Junior Rodeo for Goliad County. A pair of scarred ballet slippers. A sheet of music she'd played in a piano recital. A dried rose taken from her father's coffin.

There were many more bits and pieces of her life scattered across the shelves and as she gazed at them, she tried to rein in her exploding emotions. Her parents had given her a wonderful childhood and opened doors to any path she'd wanted to take. These years she'd been away, she'd not stopped to think that her family might be expecting her to eventually give back to the ranch. Instead, she'd been selfishly focused on her own career.

"If you're trying to make me feel guilty, Mother, then you've certainly succeeded," she murmured hoarsely.

Mercedes had hardly gotten the words out when she felt her mother's hands on her shoulders, gently pulling her around.

"Mercedes!" she scolded softly. "I'm not trying to make you feel guilty. I'm sorry if I did. But I *am* trying to jar you. To wake you up out of this foggy sleep you've been in ever since you left the Sandbur."

Pressing her lips to a firm line, Mercedes swung her head back and forth. Eight years ago, shortly after she'd learned the truth about John, she'd met an Air Force recruiter on campus. He'd made the idea of serving her country and acquiring a new career sound exciting and challenging, just what she'd needed to take her mind off the miserable mistakes she'd made. Initially, she supposed she had used the military as a way to get away from campus and the Sandbur. She'd had her fill of her family watching her with sympathy and treating her as though she had an illness instead of a broken heart. But once she'd gotten through basic training at Lackland Air Force Base, her whole attitude toward her enlistment had taken on a different meaning. Now, her service as an airman was important to her and was something she was definitely proud of. The past eight years had shaped and strengthened her. She wanted her mother and the rest of her family to see that she could bear up under any pressure.

"I've hardly been living in a coma," she muttered.

Geraldine rolled her eyes. "Okay, maybe I should have said you've been hiding in your job. You loved being on Diego Garcia because the tiny island was totally away from the rest of the world. Away from the rest of us regular folks doing the mundane task of living. I actually think if you'd been given the choice, you would have stayed there forever."

Her mother's mistaken assumptions fueled Mercedes's temper. If she'd wanted to stay, as her mother had so bluntly suggested, she could have reenlisted. More than that, she could have easily continued to make the Air Force her career. But her heart had been crying out to come home. It had been longing for more than simply going through each day carrying out her duties as an airman. She'd thought her mother understood, but apparently she didn't. Mercedes couldn't stop herself from raising her voice, "And what the hell do you think I was doing there? Drinking margaritas and strumming a guitar beneath a palm tree?"

Temper sparked in Geraldine's eyes. "Your job. While conveniently forgetting the rest of your life."

Mercedes stared at her, aghast that their conversation had escalated into such a verbal war. Over the years, the two of them had argued before, but this time Geraldine's barbed words stung her worse than ever.

Mercedes was wondering what to say, or if she should even make any sort of retort, when her mother solved the problem by turning and walking out of the room.

Her eyes stinging with tears, Mercedes went over to the closet and pulled out her favorite pair of old cowboy boots. She had to get out of the house. She needed to see the ranch and remember why it had pulled her back to Texas in the first place.

Later that afternoon, Gabe stepped out of the horse barn carrying a saddle on his shoulder when the sound of cantering hoofbeats caught his attention. He looked around to see Mercedes and her mount flying toward the ranch yard. Dust boiled behind the blue roan as she steered him toward a nearby corral, then skidded the animal to a stop a nose-length away from the board fence.

His jaw slack, Gabe watched her leap from the saddle and land on the ground like an agile cat. Coming from a ranching background, he'd expected Mercedes to be able to ride, but not like Annie Oakley! Was there anything the woman couldn't do?

He walked over to one of the wranglers working in the yearling pen. "Hey, James, is that Mouse that Ms. Saddler is riding?" he asked.

The young cowboy glanced up from the rope halter he was trying to untangle and stared across the pen to where Mercedes was now slowly leading the horse around in a large circle.

"Yep, that's him. She took off on him this mornin' sometime before lunch."

Gabe silently cursed. The horse was definitely a beauty, with a blue roan coat and flax mane and tail. Part Thoroughbred, he was long and tall, as well as fast, nervous and totally unpredictable. Mouse still needed hours more training to be trustworthy for any rider, including himself.

"Did you catch him for her?"

"Nope." Glancing around at Gabe, the cowboy shook his head with a bit of admiration. "She picked him out of the *remuda* we'd rounded up for today's work and roped him herself."

Gabe stared at the ranch hand. Plenty of Texas women knew their way around a horse, but not many he knew could handle a rope, especially a loop that was tossed backward to keep the line from tightening and choking the animal. "She roped Mouse?"

"That's what I said. She threw one of the prettiest houlihans I'd ever seen before. Surprised the heck out of me. I mean, she's the boss's daughter, but she looks so delicate. I figured she'd always had her mounts saddled for her. And I dang sure never seen a girl throw a houlihan before. But she did. Then saddled him herself and took off toward the river. After that, I didn't worry about Mouse being too much horse for her. She handled him better than I could."

Gabe's gaze left the cowboy to settle on Mercedes, who was continuing to carefully cool down the horse. Since the moment he'd met her, she'd surprised him, amazed him, even worried him and now he had to admit that she wasn't the spoiled princess he'd expected her to be. Yet she *was* trouble. He could feel it stirring in his gut, whispering in his ear.

"I guess I could have tried to stop her from riding Mouse," James went on. "But she didn't look like she was in any mood to take advice from me. I warned her that he was high-strung. That's about all I could do."

Gabe dropped an understanding hand on James's shoulder. "Don't worry about it," he told the cowboy, then walked over to the fence. After he unloaded the saddle on the top rail, he headed straight to Mercedes.

By the time he reached her, she had tied Mouse to a hitching post and was working loose the back cinch from beneath the animal's underbelly. As Gabe came to a stop a few feet from where she was standing, she tossed him a stoic glance.

"Good evening," she greeted.

He inclined his head politely toward her. "Evenin'," he replied as his eyes slid over the curves hidden behind her white shirt and dark blue jeans. It was hard to believe that he'd had that perfect body crushed against his, that he'd tasted the sweet wine of her lips.

Not bothering to say more, she continued to unsaddle the horse. Gabe studied her for long moments and wondered why he couldn't stay away from her. He didn't like to think of himself as weak willed, but she definitely made him feel out of control.

After a bit, he stated the obvious. "I see you've been riding Mouse."

"Is that his name?"

"Nickname."

"Not a very good one," she said. "Because he's not afraid of anything."

Apparently she wasn't, either, Gabe thought. Stepping closer, he said, "Did he give you any problems?"

She glanced at him as though she found his question surprising. "None at all. He's a honey horse. I really like him."

As though to emphasize her words, she stroked the animal's sweaty neck. As Gabe's gaze followed the movement of her small hand, he couldn't help but remember the way it had touched him, the way it had tasted when he'd kissed the back of it.

"Then Mouse must like you better than he likes the cowboys here on the ranch. He's usually a devil. A few weeks ago, he tossed one of the hands and broke the guy's collarbone."

She hefted the saddle from the horse's back and lifted it

onto the top rail of the fence. It wasn't like Gabe to stand still and allow a woman to do such manual labor, but he instinctively understood that she didn't want or require his help. She was just the sort of independent woman that enjoyed showing a man she didn't need him. The same way Sherleen had taken pleasure in reminding him how easily she could get along without him, he thought sourly.

"Mouse knew that I trusted him," Mercedes said. "And that's all he needed to trust me back."

Gabe would have never expected this woman to understand a horse's psyche. The fact that she did impressed him, in spite of himself.

Clearing his throat, he said, "Uh, Mercedes, I'm glad I saw you ride up. I think— I want to apologize to you."

Twisting her head, she peered skeptically at him. "You *think* you want to apologize? Or you *know* that you want to apologize?"

He moved closer, until the scent of horse and woman mingled and swirled beneath his nostrils.

With a rueful grimace, he said, "I want to apologize. I was out of line this morning. I had no right or reason to—uh—grab you the way I did in the office. You were only teasing and I should have took it as such."

He watched her blue eyes widen with surprise. Her whole body turned to face him.

"Do you really mean that?" she asked softly.

Gabe could feel his heart jerk, then take off in a hard gallop. God, but this was crazy. No woman, including his ex-wife, had ever affected him this much. He'd thought about her all day. All day.

"I really mean it," he said.

She let out a long breath, smiled briefly, then quickly

dropped her head. A few moments passed before Gabe realized she was crying. Seeing her in such a vulnerable state stunned him, tore him like the tip of a lashing whip.

"Mercedes?" he asked softly, then carefully placed a hand on her shoulder. "What's wrong?"

Blinking back her tears, she lifted her eyes to his face. "Forgive me, Gabe. I—I don't normally behave as though I'm having an emotional breakdown."

His fingers tightened and unconsciously began kneading her shoulder. "I didn't mean to hurt you. Forget what I said this morning."

She sucked in a deep breath. "It's not you. Although I'm glad we're not at war with each other. It would be pretty awful for the two of us to circle each other like mad dogs every time we crossed paths."

"Yeah. Someone might have wanted to shoot the both of us," he teased.

She tried to smile, but fresh tears spilled from her eyes. The urge to pull her into his arms and kiss those tears away rushed over him like a sudden, unexpected rainstorm. The strange reaction dazed him, making him feel worse than gullible. Hell, he'd never felt the urge to console anybody. Except maybe as a very young boy when he'd found his mother crying over the empty cupboards and unpaid bills. Yeah, he'd hugged his mother tightly and told her how much he loved her. *As if love would fix anything,* he thought bitterly. He'd tried to comfort Sherleen when she'd been upset, but she'd never been the tearful sort. She'd been a screamer and his attempts to placate her had been shunned.

Shoving that unwanted thought aside, Gabe watched Mercedes dash the tears away with the back of her hand. "I got into a quarrel of sorts with Mother this morning. I've been riding out over the range this afternoon thinking about her and the ranch and—a lot of things."

His gaze touched the sweet lines of her face. "Coming home isn't as easy as it sounds."

Mercedes realized his simple statement completely summed up the emotional turmoil inside her, and she looked at him with new regard. "Sometimes I think I've been gone too long, Gabe. Maybe I've forgotten how to be a part of this ranch."

"You haven't forgotten."

His gaze was piercing, unsettling, forcing her to look away from him and swallow.

"Mother expects me to make my home—my life—here now."

"And what do you want, Mercedes?"

She could feel his fingers cease their movement on her shoulder, as though every part of him was waiting for her answer. Could it really matter to him whether she stayed on the ranch or left for parts unknown?

"I rode Mouse all the way to the river," she said quietly. "And by the time I got back here to the ranch yard, I realized how much I still love this place."

"Enough to stay?"

A wry smile touched her lips. She'd already made up her mind that the Sandbur was her home now, but she wasn't comfortable sharing that information with Gabe just yet. It was hard enough for her to have a simple conversation with him. "You'll have to ask me that later, Gabe. Right now I'd better go make peace with my mother."

She turned to untie the reins from the hitching post, but Gabe's hand suddenly swept hers away.

"You go find Geraldine. Let me take care of Mouse for you."

She hesitated, feeling both awkward and touched that he was being so thoughtful. Maybe he had truly put their cross words of this morning behind him. She hoped so. The sexual tension between them was more than enough to handle without adding hostility to it.

"He needs a bath," she said of the horse.

His grin was droll. "I know how to give him one."

The playful look on his face filled Mercedes with relief and a lightheartedness she'd not felt in a long, long time.

Laughing, she rose on her tiptoes and planted a kiss on his cheek. "Yes, I guess you do. Thanks, Gabe!"

As she turned and hurried away, Gabe stared after her and, like a fool, wondered how long it would be before he watched her walk away from the Sandbur. From him.

## *Chapter Four*

An hour later, freshly showered and dressed in shorts and a tank top, Mercedes came downstairs to find her mother sitting on the front porch, talking on a cell phone. Near her armchair, on a low wicker table, sat a small pitcher filled with what looked to be margaritas. Next to it was an insulated ice bucket, along with empty glasses.

Mercedes helped herself to one of the drinks, then eased down in a rocker angled to her mother's right. By the time she'd swallowed the first sip of the icy lime and tequila concoction, Geraldine had folded the phone shut and tossed it onto the table.

"That was Mrs. Richman, scolding me for not being present for the library fund-raiser last week," she said. "I was trying to explain that my daughter had just come home from a job that has kept her halfway around the world for two years, but that didn't faze the woman. I guess the five thousand dollars I contributed wasn't enough to suit her."

Geraldine sighed with frustration and Mercedes tossed her an understanding smile.

"Sounds as if things haven't changed a bit around here. Everyone is always wanting more and more from you. If not your money, then your time. I honestly don't know how you do it, Mother."

Geraldine reached up to push a hand through her hair and, not for the first time since she'd been home, Mercedes noticed that her mother no longer wore the wide gold wedding band on her left hand. Her father had been dead for eleven years and Mercedes was glad to see that her mother had moved on, but it still affected Mercedes to see the empty ring finger. To her, it signified the end of a beautiful union that had produced her and her two siblings. It also said that relationships, even the best of them, sometimes ended in tragedy. Something she was definitely acquainted with.

"You just deal with things one at a time, honey. Otherwise, I would have been be carted off to the psychiatric ward a long time ago." Turning her head, she leveled a look on Mercedes. "I'm glad to see you're in a better frame of mind than you were this morning."

Shamefaced, Mercedes dropped her gaze to the drink in her hand. As she swirled around the milky green liquid, she said, "I want to apologize for my behavior this morning, Mother. I was acting like a shrew—or a spoiled brat—or something that I shouldn't have been. I hope you'll forgive me."

Geraldine's soft laugh drifted on the muggy breeze and Mercedes lifted her head to look at her.

"You never have to ask for my forgiveness, kitten. You know that. Besides, I said some pretty harsh things to you."

"You were only trying to shake me up," Mercedes reasoned.

The faint grin on Geraldine's face faded. "Did I succeed?"

Mercedes absently plucked at the hem of her shorts. "Well, it made me realize how much I love this place and still think of it as home."

Her mother reached across the space separating their chairs to pat Mercedes's forearm.

"I always knew that, darling. But it's very nice to hear you say it." She studied her daughter's serious face. "Does this mean you've definitely decided to stay on the ranch?"

Mercedes gave her a brief nod. "It does. But only if I can be useful. I'm not a hanger-on, Mother. You know that. I never was, and I don't intend to start now. I guess—well, I've done a lot of growing up since I've been away from the ranch and this morning—I'm ashamed that you had to remind me of my responsibility as a Saddler."

Geraldine's slender fingers gently rubbed the top of Mercedes's hand. "Mercedes, if you think I was implying that you've neglected your family while you were away— well, I couldn't be sorrier. I'm proud of all that you've accomplished. The whole family is proud of you. I was only—"

"Being your blunt self," Mercedes said with a soft chuckle. "Forget it, Mother. I have. The only thing I want to hear is what I can do around here to be truly helpful—other than get in Lex's way," she added teasingly.

Leaning back in her chair, Geraldine took a long sip of her drink before she gave Mercedes a smug smile. "I have the perfect job for you, dear. We need someone to help with the marketing for the ranch. Cordero used to do some of it, but as you know, he's over in Louisiana now getting the horse farm going. And Lex doesn't have time for it. Now with us using the Internet and television to reach buyers, it's a huge job to take care of these issues. Matt is already getting ready for the second annual televised cattle auction in September and now he and Lex are making noises about doing another one with the horses. I don't know when they'll find the time, but if you pitch in, maybe they can swing it."

Mercedes's interest was more than piqued and she scooted excitedly to the edge of her seat. "That sounds great, Mother! And I'm surprised. I didn't have any idea the ranch was getting that deeply into advertising and marketing. I thought it was still just ring up a buyer on the phone and they'd show up sooner or later with a few cattle trucks to haul off what they bought."

Geraldine chuckled. "Sorry, Mercedes, but the U.S. military aren't the only ones to use high-tech devices. Your grandparents wouldn't believe how far the Sandbur has come since their heyday."

"Hmm. It sounds interesting and challenging and it's something I would love to do." But would it mean she'd have to deal with Gabe on a fairly regular basis? That might be tricky. Still, she wasn't a coward. If she had to deal with Gabe, she would.

Geraldine's grin was a bit wry. "Well, it wouldn't be like gathering information for the military. But it would be a challenge, I grant you that. Think you want to tackle it?"

Mercedes left her chair and sat on the floor next to her mother's knees. "Of course I want to tackle it." She reached for Geraldine's hands and squeezed them tightly. "And I want to thank you for not trying to manufacture some sort of job for me just as a way to make me feel needed or useful. I—I couldn't stand that."

Geraldine made a noise of disapproval. "Mercedes, you know I'm too direct to try to dance around or spin the issue. Lay things out as they really are—that's the best way to handle a problem."

Her mother's frankness when dealing with people had always been something Mercedes counted on and respected.

Sometimes her brutal honesty hurt, but painful or not, it was usually right. Geraldine hadn't been exactly on the mark when she'd accused Mercedes of wanting to stay in Diego Garcia as a way to avoid civilian life, but she'd been right that Mercedes had used her job to help push away personal disappointments.

Sighing, she rested her cheek on her mother's knee and gazed out at the front lawn of the ranch house. For the first time since she'd arrived home, she felt a sense of peace, of belonging.

Was that because of the job her mother had just offered her, a job that would truly be beneficial to the ranch and her family? Or was she feeling this spurt of happiness because of Gabe?

Even asking herself that last question seemed ridiculous. Gabe Trevino didn't have anything to do with her coming home to the Sandbur or putting a smile on her face, Mercedes told herself firmly. Even so, she still couldn't forget the wicked way he'd kissed her or the way she'd wanted to melt against him. The fact that he was here on the ranch, that she'd likely be dealing with him through her work, filled her with an excitement she'd never expected to feel again.

"Mother, do you know much about Gabe Trevino?"

Geraldine stroked a hand over her daughter's thick hair. "You mean, other than the fact that he's a wizard with horses?"

"Hmm. Where did he come from?"

"Well, from what Cordero said, the man has been traveling from coast to coast for the past few years, working mainly for wealthy horse owners. But I believe he grew up here in Texas, down south in the valley."

*Coming home isn't as easy as it sounds.* Where she was concerned, Gabe's comment had hit the mark. But now she wondered if he'd said it out of his own personal experience.

"Then settling here must be like coming home for him," Mercedes said thoughtfully.

"Guess you might say that," Geraldine replied. "Although I've not ever heard him mention having relatives anywhere close. But he did tell Lex and Matt that he was single. I suppose you're the teeniest bit interested in that detail about the man?"

Lifting her head, Mercedes countered her mother's question with a low chuckle. "Why, Mother, I wasn't asking anything of the sort. I just— Well, I was just curious about him. That's all."

With a shrewd smile, Geraldine tapped a finger on the tip of Mercedes's nose. "Okay. I admire Gabe. As an employee of the ranch and as a person. Does that tell you anything?"

Mercedes chuckled again, but deep inside she sadly wondered why she couldn't be more like her mother. "Yeah. It tells me that you're a very trusting woman."

A week later, Mercedes stood in the middle of her new workplace and surveyed the stark contrast. When she first entered it, the office that had once been Cordero's had resembled a storage room more than anything. Among the old furniture coated with an inch of sandy dirt, there'd been piles of papers and magazines intermingled with sales receipts, horse registrations and junk mail strewn around the room. Not to mention spurs, bits and leather tack that had been carried in from the horse pens and never returned to their proper places in the barn.

With her mother's help, all of the clutter had been cleared away, the dirt and grime cleaned from the windows and furniture and a new tiled floor installed, along with fluorescent overhead lights. Potted plants filled the corners and the space beneath the windows while a row of filing cabinets lined one wall and a new computer system took up most of the desktop.

Since she would be spending most of the hours of her days

here, Mercedes was very pleased with the room. It was now clean and comfortable and had everything she needed. The only thing she wasn't sure about was the wide-paned window overlooking the training pen.

The huge corral was where most of the yearlings were taught to lead, where the two-year-olds were broken to ride, and later trained to gait and neck rein. Simply put, it was where Gabe spent most of his time and where she'd caught herself gazing out to see him at work, or to see if he was anywhere near. The idea that she could glance up from her desk and most likely get a glimpse of the man was more than distracting.

In fact, she'd tried to maneuver her desk to a position where the window wouldn't be in the line of her vision, but her mother had considered her decision more than a bit odd. No normal person wanted to stare at a wall when he or she could gaze out at a crop of beautiful horses, Geraldine had told her. It had been impossible for Mercedes to explain that the wall would be easier for her peace of mind than gazing out at the sexy horseman.

Yesterday, her first official day on the job, he'd called to inform her that he needed a whole folder of information typed and sent to an auction company in North Texas. When he'd offered to bring the papers to her new office, she'd quickly put him off and offered to pick them up at his office, instead. For some ridiculous reason, she'd wanted to avoid having the man inside her small working space. She'd been afraid that his presence would be too big to ever leave and then she'd have even more trouble concentrating on her work.

Yet going to his office hadn't been a bit easier. She'd been stupid to think she could return to the scene of the crash and not be jolted all over again. She'd gotten out of there so fast, he'd still been talking as she'd backed out the door. She suspected that he knew exactly why she'd scampered like a scalded cat.

Sighing, Mercedes walked over to the desk and was about to take a seat in the wide leather chair when she noticed the papers she'd bundled together with a rubber band. The horse registrations belonged in Gabe's files, and since he had no idea they were here, it was her responsibility to deliver them.

Seeing the man again was not something she was looking forward to, but she was going to have to get accustomed to it. Horses were big business on the Sandbur, and Gabe was the boss over all things equine. Like it or not, she was going to have to deal with him and this strange attraction that came over her whenever he was near.

And with that in mind, Mercedes snatched up the papers and headed out the door.

Even though it wasn't yet nine o'clock, the morning was already hot, the air heavy with humidity. During the past few years, Gabe had worked in several different states, most of which had a much drier and more pleasant climate than South Texas. Five minutes of this weather had sweat rolling down his face and soaking his shirt. After an hour of the oppressive heat, his legs felt as though lead balls were fastened to his boots.

A smart person would never purposely choose to live here, Gabe thought, but he'd never been accused of being smart. He could have stayed in Colorado or the cool northern mountains of California, where jogging five miles never made him break a sweat. Instead, he'd chosen to come back to Texas, back to the prickly pear and thorny mesquite, where alligators ruled the rivers and rattlesnakes almost outnumbered the fire ants. Where old memories haunted him at every turn. Yeah, he'd been crazy for coming back here, but it was home—a fact that he couldn't change. Nor did he want to. And maybe, just maybe, he'd come back to Texas as a way to punish himself. After all, his parents had never gotten out of Grulla, so why should he?

Shoving that dismal question out of his head, Gabe slipped a bright green halter over the ears of a red roan filly. She was thirteen-months-old and as pretty as a calm lake beneath a full moon.

"It's all right, little darlin'," he crooned to the yearling. "We're gonna get along fine. As fine as rain in the desert."

"Good morning, Gabe."

The sudden sound of a female voice came from somewhere behind him. He glanced over his shoulder to see Mercedes sitting atop the board fence of the corral, a cupped hand shielding her eyes.

Since the day she'd ridden Mouse, he'd only seen her once and that had been yesterday, when she'd come to his office to pick up a stack of auction data. For the most part she'd been friendly and had seemed eager to do the work he asked of her. Yet he'd sensed that she was doing her best to keep plenty of distance between them. He could only guess that she'd had time to think about the kiss they'd shared and was now regretting that she'd allowed it to happen. Well, he was regretting it, too. Mainly because the memory only made him want to repeat the act.

As for her taking on the marketing job for the ranch, Gabe had been totally surprised when Lex had given him the news. Gabe had been expecting to hear she'd headed off to some high-powered job with the CIA or FBI. Instead, he'd watched building contractors move in to the old cattle barn to erect the woman a fancy office.

With the filly obediently following him, Gabe decided he didn't have much choice other than to stroll in Mercedes's direction. "Good morning," he greeted as he drew near the spot where she was sitting. "You're out early this morning."

Squinting, she lifted her eyes toward the east where the morning sun was already bearing down on the spreading live oaks. "This is late for me. I've been up for hours."

"Guess it's hard to change military habits."

She nodded, then gave him a brief smile and Gabe realized he was staring at her, his gaze eating up her fresh face with its full soft lips and dark blue eyes. Dammit, why did she have to be so beautiful, so tempting?

"Uh, I didn't want to interrupt your work. I was on my way over to your office and I spotted you here." She held up a packet of folded papers. "I wanted to give you these American Quarter Horse Association horse registrations. Cordero wasn't too good about keeping things filed. I'm not sure if we still own the horses or not. Maybe you can figure it out."

He took the papers from her, then immediately stuffed them in the back pocket of his jeans. "Thanks. I'll go through them later. Could be the buyers never picked up the papers or Cordero never mailed them out."

Gabe watched her hands slide nervously down her thighs. Today she was wearing faded jeans and a white shirt with the tails knotted in the front at her waist. Her hair was hanging loose, and he figured if he slid his hand beneath its weight and touched the back of her neck, he'd find it damp and hot. Like a few other places on her body.

She laughed softly, and Gabe felt a rush of pleasure pass through him. The sound was happy and sensual at the same time, and he found himself wondering if she would be the sort of woman who'd smile as he made love to her.

*Hell, Gabe, get your mind on your own business and off this blond siren. Her last name is Saddler, remember? She's the boss lady's daughter and that makes her a rich ranching heiress. You'd better never touch her again. Not that way.*

He said, "From what I know about Cordero, he doesn't like working under a roof, much less filing papers."

She leveled her eyes on his face, and for the first time in his life, he wondered how women—particularly this woman—saw him. The idea that she was scrutinizing him for any reason left him uncomfortable and he deliberately looked away from her and back to the roan who was standing quietly behind him. The filly's ears were perked forward, her brown eyes soft and trusting.

Warmed by the animal's faith in him, he gently stroked her slender neck while he struggled to minimize the effect Mercedes's presence had on him.

"You don't look as if you particularly enjoy being under a roof, either," she remarked.

"You're right. I've always been an outdoorsman. But I do force myself to keep up with paperwork. It's an important part of the job."

"From what my family tells me, you're filling Cordero's boots and then some. All of them are very pleased with your work."

There was a white jagged streak down the filly's nose and Gabe traced the marking with his forefinger as he carefully digested Mercedes's comment. It would be stupid as hell to let her compliments go to his head. Still, he couldn't help but ask, "What about you? Do I measure up to your standards?"

Silence stretched for long moments until it seemed that even the birds had stopped chirping. Finally she said, "I haven't been here long enough to make that judgment. But I trust my family's opinion."

Hearing a smile in her voice, he glanced over his shoulder

to see a half grin curving one side of her lips. It was a sexy expression. One that said she could be very playful if she was with the right person. And he was a damn fool for wishing that person could be him.

Without warning, she suddenly jumped into the pen and walked over to where he was standing. Her nearness surprised him. Especially after yesterday, when she'd gone overboard to keep a professional distance between them.

"What are you doing with the little filly?" she asked.

Did she really care or was she simply making conversation, trying to alleviate the obvious tension between them? *What the hell does it matter, Gabe? She's here by your side. Quit trying to figure her out and simply enjoy having her close.*

He glanced at her. "Just seeing if she'll give me her head. And yield to my pressure."

She leveled those blue eyes on him again, and this time Gabe was acutely aware that she was only a step away, close enough to pick up her scent and see the faint spatter of freckles across her cheekbones. He could feel the heat of her gaze sliding over his face, down his shoulder and onto his hands.

He could never remember a woman looking at him in such a sensual way. Or if they had, he hadn't noticed. Mercedes's slanting glances were causing fire to lick at his insides and he silently cursed the strong reaction.

She was everything in a woman he'd promised himself to avoid. Strong-minded. Independent. Wealthy. She didn't need a man on a permanent basis. And after one failed marriage, he wasn't looking to enter into another relationship that was doomed from the start.

"Does she have a name yet?"

"I call her Penny." In spite of the mental argument he'd just made with himself, every cell inside Gabe was urging him to step closer, to enjoy the heat she was throwing at him. But he stopped himself short.

She glanced beyond him and the filly to an adjoining pen where ten more yearlings were waiting to go through a morning of schooling.

"How do you keep them all straight? And where do you find enough time to give them all the handling they need?"

Instead of following her gaze to the other young horses, he allowed his eyes to travel over the graceful line of her profile, the curve of her throat and the thick waves of her long hair. Even though she was everything he didn't need, she had everything he wanted.

"I have several wranglers that I trust to deal with the young horses in the way I insist upon. As for the horses themselves, they're just like humans—they all have different personalities that make them unique. Like Penny here, who's sweet and docile and is willing to do anything I ask of her."

Mercedes smiled perceptively. "Hmm. She must be a favorite of yours."

"She is. But I'd say a bit of fire added to all that sweetness isn't a bad thing."

Mercedes cleared her throat as the subtle undercurrent of his words splashed heat across her cheeks. She'd not stopped to flirt with the man. She'd simply wanted to deliver the papers, pause long enough to appear friendly, then head back to work. Yet it seemed that whenever she got near him, her brain seemed to lose control of her body. As for him, Mercedes wasn't sure how to take anything he said. But then, she'd stopped believing in men a long time ago.

"If that's the case, you should have supper with us tonight," she impulsively blurted out before she could stop herself.

"Cook is grilling steaks. I'm sure she'd supply you with all the Tabasco you need."

Dear God, where had that come from and what had she been thinking? Being around this man was like striking matches near a puddle of gasoline. For the past few days, she'd been convincing herself that the safe thing to do would be to forget his kiss and keep everything friendly and professional between them. But for some reason she couldn't fathom, the risk, the pure excitement of being in his company was too much to resist.

Mercedes could see he was carefully weighing her invitation, as though he didn't trust her nearly as much as he did the little roan filly nuzzling his shoulder. She didn't understand why he would be skeptical about her sincerity, but after years of information gathering for the military, she'd learned that outright questions rarely provided as many answers as sitting back and observing. Sooner or later, she'd figure out what lay beneath Gabe Trevino's dark eyes and why he thought she had a hidden agenda where he was concerned.

"I'm not sure that's a good idea," he said finally.

Disappointment speared through her…which was a ridiculous reaction on her part. Her happiness didn't depend on this man liking her or her company. In fact, she'd most likely be better off if he did decline her invitation. Still, her heart was beating with an eagerness that frightened her.

"Why? Don't you eat in the evening?"

"Yes. But—"

"Then there are no buts," she quickly interrupted with a smile. "I'll tell Cook to set another plate. We eat around seven."

Before he could issue another objection, she turned on her heel and hurried to climb out of the horse pen. Once she'd reached the top rail, she looked back at him and waved. "Oh, and don't dress up," she called out. "This is just a family affair."

\* \* \*

Later that evening, Gabe stood on his front porch and stared out at the rough ground dotted with scrubby oak and mesquite. The house where he'd settled on the Sandbur had once been little more than a line shack. A three-room building with a rusted iron roof and a separate outhouse for bathroom facilities. Just a spot for line riders to rest and find shelter from the weather.

Over the years, it had been updated and expanded. A well had been dug, electricity added and the house modernized with indoor plumbing. Even so, the place felt isolated and hidden from the rest of the world.

Almost five miles away from the main ranch yard, the homestead sat on a brushy knoll that angled down to the banks of the San Antonio River. Sometimes a few cows would appear in the yard to graze around the patches of prickly pear, or deer and wild turkey would stroll by to feed at the dry corn he tossed beneath the lone pine tree standing in front of the house. But other than the wildlife, he didn't hear or see anyone. It was just him and the wind. And he liked it like that.

At first, Geraldine and Matt had thought he was kidding when he'd told him he wanted to move his things into this empty house. No one had used it in several years and the ranch had much better places to offer as living quarters.

Gabe had finally convinced them that he was serious about making the old house his home. But before he could move his things in, Geraldine had set a contractor to work installing wood parquet on the floors and exchanging the old appliances in the kitchen with new ones. Thankfully, she'd left everything else as it had been and Gabe could truthfully say that this was the first place, since his childhood home in Grulla, where he felt comfortable.

At least, he'd felt comfortable until Mercedes had made an appearance on the ranch, he thought soberly. Now thoughts and images of the woman were invading his private space and that unsettled him more than anything had in a long time.

*A family affair.* Those three words were enough to tell Gabe he didn't belong at the Saddler supper table. But he could hardly call the house with some feeble excuse and tell them he didn't want to be there. Dammit, why had she asked him, anyway?

The question had rolled through Gabe's head all afternoon, but now it was too late to be asking himself anything. He had no choice but to get ready and go. And later, before the evening was through, he had to get the message across to Mercedes Saddler that he wasn't interested in socializing, or anything else, with her.

## Chapter Five

At the same time in the Saddler house, Mercedes had gone to the kitchen to remind Cook to set another plate for supper and had just received a shock from the older woman.

"Honey, there's no need to be adding another plate. One ought to do it. Your mother is already gone for the evenin'. She had some sort of dinner thing with the volunteer firefighters going on. I thought you knew that. And Lex has gallivanted off to some Cattle Association meetin' up at Fort Worth. He won't be back home for three days."

Mercedes stared blankly at Cook, a tall slender woman in her midseventies, who'd worked at the Sandbur for longer than Mercedes had been alive. Her long hair, which was still more black than gray, was oftentimes pulled into a tight ponytail, a style that Cook called her instant face-lift. But it was her red lips and fingernails that were her signature fashion statement, telling the world that the woman had been a glamor gal in her prime.

"I just talked to Mother this morning—before I went to work," Mercedes explained with frustration. "She didn't mention the firefighter thing. If she did, I didn't remember. And when did Lex decide to go to Fort Worth? It's funny that you know all about these things and I don't."

"That's what you get for puttin' your office way out there in the cattle barn. If you'd stayed here in the house, you might know what was going on."

That was true. But that still wouldn't have prevented her from seeing Gabe, she thought with a prickle of nerves. She'd had to deliver those damn papers.

*But that didn't mean you had to invite him to dinner, Mercedes. So why did you? So you might have the chance to spend time exclusively with the man?*

Purposely shoving that question aside, Mercedes rolled her eyes at Cook. "I put my office in the cattle barn so that I'd have enough peace to concentrate. Besides, I know I didn't misunderstand you this morning when you said that you were going to be grilling steaks for supper."

"I did say that. Before I knew that more than half the family was going to be gone."

Mercedes groaned. "Cook! I've invited Gabe to eat with us tonight! I told him we'd be having steaks!"

Cook took a step back and surveyed Mercedes with new interest. "Gabe, is it? You settin' your eye on the ranch's new horseman?"

Mercedes was astonished to feel a blush creeping up her throat and onto her cheeks. She was a grown woman who'd lived halfway around the world. For the past eight years, she'd worked in situations which could be described as stressful or worse. Nothing, other than Drew Downy's betrayal, had fazed her. Now Gabe, or the mere mention of the man, was enough to shake her nerves and color her face.

"No! I…just happened to be talking to him this morning and wanted to be sociable and invite him to supper, that's all. He's…well, he's all alone and I figured he might like a bit of company."

Cook's dark eyes glinted mischievously. "Hmmph. There's a whole bunkhouse full of beer-drinkin', poker-playin' cowboys out back. The man can find all the company he needs right there."

Mercedes frowned. "Gabe is more…refined than that."

Cook laughed. "Honey, there ain't no man on this ranch more refined than that," she said. Then, her expression more serious, she reached over and patted Mercedes's shoulder. "Don't look so glum. I'm only teasing. I think it's nice that you asked Gabe to supper. He don't have any family around here and he lives alone, way out there in the line shack. Did your mother tell you that?"

Surprised by this news, she looked at the older woman. "No one told me. I took it for granted that he probably lived in one of the newer houses here near the ranch yard."

Cook shook her head. "He's independent, I'll say that." She narrowed a shrewd gaze at Mercedes. "Sorta like you."

Mercedes straightened her spine. "I'll take that as a compliment. Now what about supper? Can you still prepare the steaks?"

Cook batted a hand through the air. "Sure. No problem. I'll make something hearty to go with them. You wanna eat in the dining room?"

Mercedes thought about that for a moment. "No. That's too stuffy for just the two of us. I'll fix a table out on the patio. What do you think?"

Cook's laugh was suggestive. "I think you're wantin' to be more than sociable."

Groaning, Mercedes hurried out of the kitchen before Cook could say more.

An hour later, she'd changed into a short denim skirt and a sheer pink blouse with a lacy camisole beneath it. After twisting up her hair in a knot at the back of her head and swiping on a bit of pink lipstick, she hurried downstairs to locate a table to use on the patio.

She found a card table in the den and covered it with a checked tablecloth from the kitchen pantry. By the time she'd added dishes, cutlery and candles, she heard a vehicle pulling up to the parking area at the west end of the house.

It had to be Gabe. She walked across the yard to the end of the two-story hacienda-style house, and as she rounded the corner, she spotted him climbing down from the cab of a black pickup truck.

He was dressed basically the way he'd been dressed this morning, only minus the spurs. Even his black hat was still wearing dust from the horse lot, yet as she came nearer, she could see that he'd shaved and his dark hair was damp and shiny.

Her gaze slid over his hard, trim body, and she felt desire gurgle in the pit of her stomach, like fire being stoked beneath an already simmering cauldron. The idea that she could feel like a whole woman again was both exhilarating and frightening.

"Hello," she called out to him.

Spotting her, he paused long enough for her to join him.

"I wasn't expecting you to meet me outside," he said.

She laughed. "I was already out back," she explained. "I heard you drive up."

Forgetting her plan to keep distance between them, she

threaded her arm around his and began to lead him toward the backyard. "I hope you don't mind, I've set a table on the patio for our supper. But if you'd rather, we can move inside to the dining room."

Gabe tried not to notice the way she was holding his arm or the way her curvy body brushed against his side as they walked. He tried to ignore the scent of her perfume and the fact that he could see through her blouse to the intimate garment beneath. But his attempts were so feeble that his senses were instantly overcome with her presence.

"I think you should be worrying about where your family would prefer to eat instead of asking me. I can eat anywhere. Standing up, or in the saddle, if necessary."

She looked at him and smiled. "That won't be necessary tonight. And as for my family, I'm afraid it's going to be only you and me. Mother had to go out this evening and Lex has gone to Fort Worth on business."

He felt as though someone had struck him over the head and it took him a moment to recover from her announcement. "Oh. You should have called me."

"Why? So you could have backed out and left me to eat all by myself?" Dimples curved the sides of her lush lips. "No. I wasn't going to give you that chance." She urged him forward. "Come on. I'll let Cook know you're here and then we'll have a drink."

Once they reached the patio, she invited him to take a seat. While she hurried into the house, Gabe walked under the vine-covered roof and stood looking at the cozy little table set for two. The fact that she'd gone to this much trouble for him was both puzzling and touching. Moreover, he couldn't figure this sudden change in her attitude or why she was bothering with him in the first place.

She was a Sandbur heiress. She could have any man she wanted.

*She doesn't want you, Gabe. Not the way you're thinking. She's only being sociable. Like her mother. Or else she's only playing with you.*

Trying to forget about Mercedes's motives, Gabe turned and strolled away from the patio to where the short-cropped lawn grew beneath the arms of a spreading live oak. A wrought iron bench sat near the massive trunk and Gabe sat on it while he waited for his hostess to reappear.

He was watching a couple of fox squirrels battle with a group of mockingbirds over a feeder full of seeds when Mercedes finally reappeared from the house, carrying a tray.

As soon as he spotted her walking toward him, he found himself wondering what he was doing here. Dreaming? Pretending that the long-legged beauty smiling at him could actually be more than a friend to him? *Get real, Gabe. Sherleen already taught you a good, hard-learned lesson about high-maintenance women and trying to keep them satisfied. Even if you could have her, you know you'd never be able to keep her contented.*

Rising to his feet, he walked across the lawn to meet her.

"I brought ice-cold beer and wine so you can take your pick. Or if you don't want spirits, I'll go back for fruit juice." She grinned impishly at him. "I'm saving the sweet tea to go with our supper."

He plucked a long-necked bottle of beer from the tray. "This will be fine. Thanks."

"Let me put this down and we can go back under the tree if you'd like," she said. "I think it's cooler there. There's not much air stirring tonight."

He waited while she put the tray on a small table on the

patio. When she returned to his side, she was carrying a beer for herself. That surprised him. He'd figured her for light wine or a fruity cocktail. But he was quickly learning that Mercedes was not a predictable woman.

They walked over to the wrought iron bench and he waited for her to take a seat before he sat down next to her. Since the piece of furniture was small, he couldn't put much space between them and he wondered if she was as intensely aware of his body as he was of hers.

"I hope you're not completely starving. Once Cook learned that I was the only one who'd be home this evening, she let the help off with plans to give me a salad. I had to remind her that I don't eat like my sister, Nicci. I want something I can really bite into. And it shows," she added with a laugh. "But I don't care. I like having healthy, strong muscles."

And he liked all the curves, Gabe could have told her. Instead he stuck to the point. "I'm not starving. And I'm sorry that Cook had to go to extra trouble for me."

She waved dismissively. "It's no trouble. She loves what she does. Besides, I've promised to clean up the kitchen for her."

Gabe's gaze slid to her hands, lightly cupped around the glass bottle balanced on her knee. Like her legs, her fingers were long, but not skinny. The bare nails were short and squared at the corners. He couldn't imagine them dipping into dirty dishwater, but he could surely imagine them sliding over his chest, down his back and onto his hips.

He let out a long breath. "You mentioned your sister, Nicci. I met her right after I came to work for the ranch and spoke to her at the party the other night. She's the PA, isn't she?"

Smiling, Mercedes nodded. "That's right. She's the brains of the family. Lex and I always had to work to keep up with the grades she made in school. It came easy to her."

"You never had the desire to follow her into the medical field?"

She laughed lowly. "Gosh, no. I don't have the patience. When I was growing up, I was too much of a tomboy, I suppose, to think of becoming a doctor. That would have required me to stay indoors and study, something I've learned to like after getting in the military. But back then I was the cowgirl and Nicci was the student." She paused and let out a sigh so soft he barely picked up the sound. "Now she has a doctor husband and a beautiful baby daughter. Have you seen Sara Rose?"

"No, but I've seen Matt's little boy. And Cordero's son."

She smiled briefly, then went very quiet for a few long moments. Gabe wondered what she was contemplating and why the mention of the children had put such a pensive look on her face. But he didn't ask. Something that personal was none of his business.

Glancing out to the feeder, he noticed the shadows had lengthened, sending the birds and the squirrels to their nightly resting places. Beyond the yard and the graceful arms of the spreading oaks, he could hear the distant sounds of male voices and the intermittent clang and thumps of a horseshoe game down at the bunkhouse.

Eventually, she turned her head slightly to look at him. "Do you have siblings, Gabe?"

Nodding, he swirled the remaining beer in the bottle he was holding. "Three. Two sisters and a brother."

Clearly curious, she squared her knees around so that she was facing him. "Really? I'm surprised. I thought—for some reason I pictured you being an only child."

"I'm the youngest." His lips twisted to a wry line. "If you can still call thirty-five young."

"I call it that," she said. Then, after swallowing a sip of her drink, she spoke again. "Tell me about them. Do they live around here?"

"No. My sisters are the oldest and after they married, they both moved away. Nita lives in Colorado now, near Cortez. Carla lives in Nevada. They both have children."

"What about your brother?"

"Joseph is three years older than me and divorced. He owns a ranch in California now—just north of Lone Pine."

"So they all live away," she mused aloud. "Do you ever see them?"

"Sometimes. Not too often." He shrugged. "When we were all children, we were very close. But then we all became adults and life took us on different paths. I think—well, if our parents had lived, we would have all remained closer."

He could feel her going very quiet again and he glanced up to see her studying him with a solemn expression.

"Your father is dead, too?"

An old, familiar pain drifted through his chest and he wondered how many years it would take for that hollow ache inside him to leave. Twenty-four had already passed and yet the time hadn't extinguished the agony of losing them. The pain was still there, haunting and hurting him anytime he thought of his loving parents.

"Yes. They both died when I was eleven."

"Oh. That's tough. Real tough," she murmured. "I guess someone has probably already told you that my father died about twelve years ago. I still miss him terribly. But I think it's worse for Lex. A man needs his father for so many reasons—that's something you know about far more than me. And it doesn't help Lex or any of the family to think Daddy might have been murdered."

Gabe's eyes narrowed on her face. "Murdered? I haven't heard anyone say anything like that about your father."

She swallowed down more of the beer. "That's because none of the family goes around saying such things to anyone. But I think—well, Mother never was convinced that the investigators did a thorough job on the case. You see, Daddy was out on a fishing trip with his friends down near Corpus. Apparently, he fell overboard with a heart attack and drowned before they could pull him back into the boat. Trouble is, Daddy didn't have an ounce of heart trouble. He'd just had a thorough checkup only weeks before the accident."

So this woman had tragically lost a parent, too, Gabe thought. He would have never guessed. For some reason, he'd always thought of families like the Saddlers and Sanchezes as never having problems or suffering losses. Which was foolish on his part. He knew firsthand that wealth didn't fix everything. It didn't necessarily bring happiness, either.

"Sometimes doctors miss problems."

"Yeah. Sometimes," she murmured, then suddenly rose to her feet. "I think I'll go check with Cook and see if our meal is ready."

"Sure. Take your time."

Fifteen minutes later, Mercedes and Gabe were sitting at the little table on the patio. Above their heads, honeysuckle vines were dripping with blossoms and filling the heavy evening air with their pungent scent. Nearby, torches burned to ward away mosquitoes.

On the table, wedged around the flickering candles, there was a platter of thick beef steaks that had been marinated, then coated with coarse black pepper and grilled to perfection. There was a bowl of pan-fried potatoes and onions, along with another bowl filled with baked beans heavily spiced with chili powder. Beneath a cloth-covered basket, sourdough biscuits were hot from the oven.

Gabe couldn't remember ever eating food that tasted so good—yet he was distracted from each delicious bite by the sight of Mercedes sitting across from him.

Except for the flickering candlelight and nearby torches, black shadows cloaked them in darkness, reminding Gabe that the two of them were entirely alone. Even the faint lights from the back of the hacienda had gone out and the muted sounds from the distant bunkhouse were now quiet.

Before Gabe had driven to the ranch yard, this was not the sort of meal he'd envisioned having with Mercedes. He'd expected to be eating in the Saddlers' elegant dining room with the whole family present. The last thing he'd anticipated was this intimate tête-à-tête.

He was washing a piece of steak down with a swig of tea and asking himself if he would have accepted her invitation if he'd known how the evening was going to turn out, when her voice broke softly into his rambling thoughts.

"I guess you're probably thinking I put these candles out here to make the dinner a romantic affair."

He looked across the short space at her and felt his gut twist with desire. The glow of the candlelight gave her skin a pearly sheen and her lips, which had been covered in pink lipstick, were now bare and moist. The memory of kissing them was still fresh in his mind. So fresh that the taste of her lips overpowered the flavor of the food on his plate.

"Did you?" he asked.

Her gaze met his in a subtle, but challenging way. "Not really. They're citronella—I didn't want us to become supper for the mosquitoes."

Her response was so unexpected that he had to laugh. "You've put me at ease."

A broad smile spread her lips. "Good. Because—well, this morning, when I first invited you to have supper with us, I hadn't planned on this." She waved her hand to encompass the table and patio. "But then, when I learned it was going to be just you and me I decided I wanted to make it a little special. Can I say that?"

He gave her a wry grin. "You just did."

She shot him a playful frown. "I mean, can I say that without making you angry?"

He shrugged. "I'm not a bit angry. Do I look like I am?"

"No. You look…skeptical. And that doesn't make me feel very good."

He forked a morsel of steak to his mouth. "I didn't know I was supposed to be making you feel good."

She let out a long breath. "All right. I'll just come out and say what I was trying to say in the first place—I wanted to show you that I like you, but I'm not trying to seduce you."

He slowly chewed the steak, then swallowed before he finally replied, "Even if you're not *trying* to seduce me—you are."

She let out a small gasp, and even in the dim light he could see her cheeks were turning dark with color. The fact that she was capable of blushing charmed him even more.

"Lord, Gabe, I never expected you to say something like that to me," she said in a low, hoarse voice.

"I don't know why," he pointed out. "You say what's on your mind to me."

She leaned back in her chair and folded her arms protectively against her breasts. For the first time since he'd met this beauty, Gabe wondered if she was really more innocent than she pretended to be.

"Well, that's because it seems like the only way I can deal with you," she reasoned.

He smiled as his eyes slid over her flustered face. "Tell me, Mercedes, have you ever had a lover?"

Surprise parted her lips and then she purposely looked away from him. "Is that question really necessary between us? I thought we were going to try to be friends."

"I don't believe we'll ever get that done."

Her gaze jerked back to his and she opened her mouth to speak, but caught herself at the last moment. Finally, she said, "Okay, since you asked, I'll tell you. I have had a lover. One. And he—well, after him I haven't wanted another."

Something about the way she spoke, the tremor in her voice, made Gabe wish he'd not asked about her past. Yet this woman consumed his thoughts and he wanted to know her. Inside and out. "Was this guy recently in your life or did it happen a long time ago?"

She looked down at her plate. "A long time ago."

"And you haven't wanted another man in your life because you still love him? Or because he twisted you?"

Twisted. Oh, yes, John had done that and much more, Mercedes thought ruefully. He'd shaken her self-esteem and made her doubt her own judgment. He'd blackened everything she'd believed love would or could be. And then, just when she'd begun to get over him, she'd met Drew and started to believe once again that men could be trusted. What a hell of a mistake that had been.

"I certainly don't love him anymore. So I guess you could say he sorta ruined my image of men in general."

"Well, don't feel alone," he said. "I think we all have our images of the opposite sex ruined at one time or another. Mine was when my wife and I divorced."

Stunned, Mercedes leaned toward him. "You were—married?"

The incredulous sound of her voice put another wry twist to his lips. "For three years."

Three years! She couldn't imagine this man being tied down for three days, much less that length of time. Apparently he'd changed since then, or he'd been wildly in love with the woman. A thought that she didn't want to contemplate.

It was silly, she knew, but after kissing the man, she was beginning to get the faintest twinges of possessiveness where he was concerned. No doubt that would give him a laugh, she thought grimly.

"What happened?"

His steak finished, he laid his fork to the side of his plate. "We had different aims in life. She couldn't live the way I wanted. And I couldn't live the way she needed. We were doomed from the start. It just took me a while to realize it."

She studied his smooth expression and wondered what was hidden behind it. Outwardly, he seemed indifferent to his failed marriage, but who knew? Maybe the man was still in love with his ex-wife. It was a notion she refused to think about.

"Uh, did you—have children?"

He shook his head. "No. Thank goodness there was no one else to be hurt by our parting."

He went quiet after that, and so did Mercedes. He'd given her much to think about. Too much.

After a while she put down her fork and settled back in her chair. "Cook tells me that you're living out at the line shack. Well, that's what we've always called it even after it was turned into a house." A tentative smile tilted the corners of her lips. "When are you going to invite me out to see it?"

She watched as his thumb and forefinger bracketed his

chin in a thoughtful pose. He was probably thinking her question was forward. It probably was. But something about this man made things tumble from her mouth that she normally wouldn't dream of saying.

"Now how am I supposed to answer that question?" he asked.

A low chuckle rumbled in her throat and she realized he was the first man other than a relative in a long, long time to make her laugh. "You're suppose to say, 'Mercedes, I'd be glad for you to come out and see the house anytime you like.'"

His eyes narrowed but not enough to hide the gleam in their gray depths. The glimmer stirred her pulse.

"Oh. Okay. Mercedes, I'd be glad for you to come out and see the house anytime you like."

"Really?"

"I said it, didn't I?"

"You were prompted."

"I said it anyway."

God, but he was stoic and frustrating, she thought. He was also too sexy to be legal. Just looking at him left her simmering and picturing the two of them in the most erotic situations. In all of her imaginings, she'd never dreamed that coming home to the Sandbur would be like this.

"All right," she told him with far more confidence than she felt. "I just might surprise you one evening with a visit."

He picked up his fork and began to draw absent lines through the crumbs on his plate. "You might be disappointed. I haven't done anything to the house, except move my things into it. I'm not one for frills and curtains and that sort of thing."

"I'd be disappointed if you were," she replied with a grin, then added, "The line shack has always been one of my favorite places on the ranch. I went out there and stayed a few days before I left for basic training."

Surprise flickered across his face. "By yourself?"

"Yes. By myself. That's the whole point of the line shack. It's away from everything and everybody. Is that why you like it?"

"Maybe."

There was no maybe about it, Mercedes thought. The man was a loner. But why, she wondered. Had losing his wife made him want to retreat from society? Or was it simply his nature to prefer his own company to others?

One way or another, Mercedes planned to find out.

## Chapter Six

As moments passed, Mercedes began to sense that he didn't appreciate her throwing questions at him, so as they finished the last of their meal, she decided to move on to other things.

"Cook made blueberry pie for dessert. Would you like to go inside and have a piece? I'll make coffee to go with it."

He rested a hand against his midsection. "I'm not sure I can hold another bite."

Rising to her feet, she began to gather up the dirty dishes. She should probably let the evening end. But this time with Gabe had been far more pleasant than she'd expected, and to be honest with herself, she didn't want to say good-night. "Cook will be very hurt if she shows up in the morning and finds the pie uncut," she told him.

"Put that way, I can't turn it down," he conceded. "Let me help you carry these into the house."

Fifteen minutes later, the dishes were piled in the sink, the coffee was made and they were sitting at the kitchen table, eating the first few bites of pie, when the swinging doors pushed open and Geraldine walked in.

"Why, Gabe! How nice to find you here!" she exclaimed as she hurried toward them. "I thought I was going to find Mercedes in here going through the refrigerator. She's a night raider."

Gabe stood up to greet Geraldine, but when he stuck out his hand toward her, she pushed it away and laughed. "I don't want a handshake from you, I want a hug."

As her mother pulled Gabe against her, Mercedes could see that the physical affection left him both awkward and surprised. Suddenly, she started thinking about the loss of his parents at a time when he'd needed hugs, encouragements and love. Maybe he'd never received that from anyone, she thought. Maybe he didn't know what it was like to be loved. Really loved. The notion saddened her greatly.

"I invited Gabe for supper tonight," Mercedes explained to her mother. "I didn't know you and Lex were going to be gone."

Stepping away from Gabe, Geraldine went over to the cabinet counter and poured herself a mug of coffee.

"Sorry. I should have called your office and told you," she said. "The county firefighters need new equipment and we're trying to come up with ideas on how to pay for them. We ranchers decided to each donate a steer, but that won't be enough. Anyway, the talking went on far too long. I'm bushed." She returned to the table and took a seat at the end of one of the long benches. "But I'm glad you and Gabe had a nice supper together. My being home would have just spoiled it."

Mercedes exchanged an awkward glance with Gabe, then cleared her throat.

"Uh, Mother, Cook made blueberry pie. Why don't you have a piece with us?"

"It's tempting. But they had donuts at the meeting. The filled kind. I ate three."

"Mother! What do you think that's done to your cholesterol?"

"Shhh! Don't tell Nicci. She'll scold me for days. Besides," she added with a pointed glance at Mercedes, "I doubt you ate rabbit food for supper."

"No," Mercedes agreed with a smile. "We had steak. And just tell Nicci what I always do. It's not the quantity of life that counts, it's the quality."

Geraldine chuckled. "See, Gabe? My daughters are nothing alike. Nicci is careful and cautious. Mercedes has always been my little daredevil."

Amused, his gaze settled on Mercedes's face. "That doesn't surprise me."

Mercedes grimaced. "I don't know why you call me a daredevil," she said to her mother. "Lex is the one who rode saddle broncs on the rodeo circuit."

"Yes," Geraldine said with a weary sigh. "And that took far more years off my heart than the damned cholesterol I eat."

From the corner of her eye, Mercedes watched Gabe glance at his watch, then push his empty pie plate to one side.

"I hate to leave good company, but it's getting late. I'd better be going," he said as he rose to his feet. "It was nice seeing you again, Geraldine."

The older woman smiled warmly at him. "I hope everything has been going okay for you here on the ranch. If you have any problems with the house, the horses, anything, just tell me. I'll fix it."

He nodded with appreciation. "Thank you. But everything is fine. No problems."

"Good." She motioned for Mercedes to get to her feet. "Where are your manners, young lady? Aren't you going to walk Gabe to his truck?"

Manners were something Geraldine had always insisted upon with her children and her employees. Short of making a scene, Mercedes had no choice but to rise to her feet. But for some reason she couldn't understand, the notion of being alone again with the man made her very nervous.

"Of course. I'll take him on the lighted path. Matt said they found two rattlesnakes on their back steps yesterday. Now he's afraid to let Juliet and the kids walk outside."

"Matt is a worrier," Geraldine said. "But it might not hurt to take a flashlight with you. There aren't any footlights on the west side of the house."

Mercedes could see very well in the darkness, but she knew better than to argue with her mother. She fetched a light from the pantry, and after Gabe wished Geraldine a good night, the two of them left the house.

Outside, Mercedes handed him the flashlight, then looped her arm around his as they followed the illuminated graveled path. But once they reached the west end, the lights faded, leaving them in total darkness.

Gabe switched on the flashlight and started to hand it back to Mercedes. "Here. I can make it the rest of the way to the truck."

"No," she told him. "We're still a good thirty feet away. A rattler might be stretched out to cool under the driver's door. I'd hate to think I was the one who caused you to get bitten."

With the orb of the flashlight pointed to the ground, the outline of his face was shrouded with shadows, but she could hear him sigh wearily. The sound bothered her. This past week, she'd come to realize that the physical attraction she felt for Gabe was only a part of what drew her to the man. For some reason she couldn't explain, she wanted him to like her as a person. She wanted to think that he savored her company rather than tolerated it. And for a while tonight, she'd believed he was enjoying spending time with her. But he was a hard man to figure.

"All right," he told her. "We'll go together."

Once they reached his truck, he paused at the door and handed the light back to her. "Thank you for the meal, Mercedes. And your company."

Strange, Mercedes thought, how just a few little words from this man had the power to lift her spirits, to make her heart trip over itself. She realized she was plunging head-first into these new feelings, but no matter how many danger signals were clanging in her head, she couldn't seem to stop them.

"Gabe, I'm sorry about Mother being so—suggestive. I don't think she realizes how transparent she is at times."

"I call it being frank."

She laughed in spite of the awkwardness between them. "Well, she does speak her mind without thinking how it sounds. And you see, for a long time now, she's been pressing me to think about marriage."

His snort was a sound of pure cynicism. "With me? You actually think your mother sees me as a potential son-in-law?"

Anger spurted through her, but she tried her best to tamp it down. So far tonight, they'd gotten along. She didn't want him to leave on a sour note. "Yes. Why? What's wrong with you?"

As the silence increased, she began to dwell on the fact that he stood only inches from her and that his warm, musky scent was filling her nostrils. Everything about the man was pulling her toward him; all she wanted to do was touch him, feel the hardness of his body beneath her hands and taste the wild passion on his lips.

"I'm not the marrying kind, Mercedes."

The sound of his voice jerked her back to their conversation. "Neither am I," she admitted. "So where I'm concerned, you don't have anything to worry about."

"Don't I?"

She sucked in a breath. It had been so long since she'd had any sort of intimate conversation with a man that maybe she was coming across in all the wrong ways. He certainly seemed to misunderstand her. "I'm not a Daisy Mae, chasing you around the hills, Gabe. And even if I were, you have two able legs. You can surely run."

She wasn't sure if he stepped closer or if she imagined it. Either way, her heart jerked with anticipation.

"You may not be Daisy Mae," he muttered wryly, "but you certainly have her…charms."

His gaze dropped from her face to slide ever so slowly down the thrust of her breasts, the curve of her waist and onto her legs, or what he could see of them in the limited light. All night he'd kept telling himself he didn't want anything from this woman. But his body was screaming it wanted to make love to her.

Mercedes's breathing sped up to such a point that she felt herself growing lightheaded.

"And that gives you a problem?" she asked.

"It does when I spend most of my waking hours imagining myself making love to you." His hand touched her hair, then settled onto her shoulder. "But then, that's what you want, isn't it? To tempt me."

Her head jerked back and forth as heat from his hand spread from her shoulder all the way to the tips of her fingers. "That's not true," she whispered hoarsely.

Suddenly his face was a breath away, his lips poised over hers. Mercedes's heart was thumping madly.

"You want me to want you," he murmured. "Don't try to deny that."

Her breaths had turned to tiny gasps, doing little to feed her oxygen-starved brain. "I'm not denying it. But I…want you to want me—like me—for…different reasons. Not the ones you're thinking."

"You just said you're not the marrying sort," he pointed out. "What other reasons could there be? Other than sex?"

Completely frustrated with him and herself, she stepped back and was about to turn in the direction of the house when he caught her upper arm and tugged her back to him.

"You didn't answer my question, Mercedes."

Her lips compressed to a thin line before she finally blurted out, "You're trying to twist everything I say and do. I'm not going to answer, or even try. You wouldn't understand."

The last three words were said with a tremor in her voice and Mercedes hated herself for showing him just how much he affected her. It wasn't right that he could twist her into knots while he appeared to be as cold as a piece of steel.

"Understand this, Mercedes. I'm a man. Not a plaything."

She struggled to keep her temper from rising and to ignore the hurt spiraling through her. But her low voice quivered with emotion when she was finally able to reply.

"Is that what you think this is all about? That I invited you here to my home because I—I want you for a sex partner? Do I look that desperate?"

No. She didn't look desperate at all, Gabe thought. Hell, she could have most any man she wanted. And that only confused him more. He couldn't understand her motives, or believe that she simply wanted his company and friendship, and it had him behaving like an ass. Yet when he looked at this woman, all he could think of was how much he wanted her and how easy it would be for him to become her fool.

"I'm sorry, Mercedes. I shouldn't have said any of that. You've been very gracious tonight. And—well, something about you brings out the worst in me." He released his hold on her arm and turned back to his truck. "I'd better go."

"Gabe."

She said his name with such soft yearning that he had to pause, had to look back.

"It's all right for me to like you, isn't it?"

"I can't think why you would."

He opened the door of the truck and climbed in. As he started the engine, he glanced out the open window to see her hovering a couple of steps away.

Lifting her hand in farewell, she called out to him, "Don't forget that I'm coming out to the line shack."

"I won't," he replied, then before he could let himself slide back to the ground and kiss her, he quickly put the truck in gear and drove away.

Three days later, Mercedes was at work in her office, downloading a series of photos she'd taken of Sandbur horses to use in a sales flier, when the door opened and her sister's head appeared.

"Nicci! Come in!"

"Are you busy? If you are, we can come back later."

"We?" Mercedes rose from behind the desk at the same time Nicci opened the door and pushed in a baby stroller.

Mercedes clapped her hands together with glee. "You've brought Sara Rose with you! How wonderful!"

Without asking permission, Mercedes immediately rushed

over to the eight-month-old child and lifted her from the stroller. "What a doll! Let me see those curls," she told the baby as she pulled a floppy pink hat from her head.

Chewing on a finger and drooling down the front of her T-shirt, Sara Rose studied her aunt with an indifferent expression, making Mercedes laugh.

"She's really impressed with me, isn't she?"

Nicci laughed. "Don't feel badly. She doesn't like just anybody. She'll hardly let Lex hold her at all. But she loves Matt."

"That's because Matt knows how to hold a real baby. Lex only knows about the grown-up females." Mercedes gestured toward the couch. "Have a seat. There are homemade cookies over by the coffee machine."

"I'll leave them alone," Nicci said, "but you might let Sara Rose chew on a half of one. It's still a while before supper."

Mercedes carried the baby over to a small table where she stored drinks and snacks and gave her half of an oatmeal cookie. Sara Rose gave the food item a hard shake, laid it on top of her head, then finally shoved it into her mouth.

"I saw another tooth!" Mercedes exclaimed. "Has she gotten another tooth?"

Nicci smiled as she settled herself on the couch. "A few days ago. I think another one on the top is coming in, too."

"Wow! The next thing I know, it'll be time for her to start nursery school."

"Please, let her start walking first," Nicci said with a good-natured groan.

Mercedes went over to the couch and sat down by her sister. After a short minute, Sara Rose began squirming and sliding off her knees, so she set the girl on the floor.

"Don't worry. It's fairly clean," Mercedes assured her sister. "No nasty boots have been in here for a while."

Nicci glanced around the neat office. "This is very nice. How do you like working for the ranch? Getting adjusted?"

"I've got to admit that it's much busier than I ever expected. In fact, I never get caught up." She gestured toward the desk where she'd been working before Nicci arrived. "I was just downloading some horse photos that have to be turned in to the auction company before noon tomorrow. I took them myself and I'm not sure if the poses show off their best points or not. I've got to show them to Gabe this afternoon so he can make the final decision about them."

Nicci's expression turned thoughtful. "Mother said you invited Gabe to supper the other night. Does that mean you're getting interested in the man?"

Leaning forward, Mercedes brushed her fingers over Sara Rose's light brown curls. "We have to work with each other and I want us to be friends. But that gets sort of complicated whenever I get around him. He's so sexy that I can hardly breathe—" She broke off as embarrassed heat colored her cheeks. "Nicci, I don't know what it is about the man. I never expected him, or any man, to make me—feel like I'm on fire."

Nicci leveled a puzzled look at her. "You used to swoon at the mention of John's name. Are you telling me this is more serious?"

Rising to her feet, Mercedes walked across the room to stare out the window overlooking the training pen. For some reason, today the wranglers had been handling the horses without Gabe overseeing them. He'd not informed her that he'd be gone. And she'd found herself glancing out the window all day for the sight of him. Her behavior made her realize she was becoming obsessed with the man. To Mercedes, that was the scariest notion of all.

"I don't know." Turning, she looked worriedly at her sister.

"Nicci, how long did it take for you to realize you—" She stopped short of using the word *love*. To imply that she was falling in love with Gabe Trevino would sound ridiculous, even to herself. "That you really cared about Ridge?"

The question caused Nicci to pause thoughtfully. "That's hard to answer. One day, it just suddenly seemed like he was all I could think about." She chuckled softly. "And that hasn't changed. He and Sara Rose are still pretty much all I think about."

Envy stabbed Mercedes as she watch Nicci's loving gaze settle on her daughter. During the past three years since Drew's betrayal, Mercedes had told herself that being a career woman was enough for her. That she could be happy without a husband or children. Yet seeing Nicci with her daughter made her hunger for a family of her own and the courage to go after her long-buried wishes.

"After all you went through with Bill, I'm surprised you were brave enough to look at another man," she commented.

Nicci shook her head. "It wasn't a matter of being brave, Mercedes. I didn't have a choice. After I met Ridge, I discovered that love wasn't something I could control. It leads you around by the nose, whether you want to be led or not."

Yes. Mercedes could believe that. The things she felt when she thought of Gabe, whenever she was near him, were beyond her control. "So what does that mean?"

Smiling impishly, Nicci answered, "It means that your heart will start overpowering your brain."

"That's a scary notion," Mercedes muttered, then walked back over to the couch and eased down next to her sister. "I can't understand it, Nicci. The man is stoic, guarded, skeptical of everything I do and say. He seems to prefer the company of horses to that of people. So why does he make my heart kick into high gear every time I see him? I really think civilian life is causing me to lose my mind."

With the cookie now little more than soggy crumbs around her mouth, Sara Rose began to crawl across the office floor straight toward a small wastebasket. Nicci jumped to her feet to go after the baby.

"Maybe it's good old-fashioned chemistry, sis," Nicci said. "My suggestion is to spend some quiet time with the man. If it's nothing more than lust, then it will burn itself out."

How could her feelings burn themselves out when Gabe wouldn't allow a flame to ever start? Mercedes tossed Nicci a dry look. "I can't even make a spark with Gabe, much less make flames. You know, sis, I'm beginning to wonder if I stayed in the Air Force too long."

Nicci chuckled as she stood Sara Rose on her feet and helped the baby balance. "What does that have to do with romance?"

Mercedes sighed. For eight years, she'd been one of the guys, a part of a team. And after Drew had cruelly used their friendship, she'd found it easy to forget she was a flesh and blood woman with needs for any sort of companionship. "Maybe I've lost my ability to attract a man."

Nicci burst out laughing. "Mercedes! You're one of the sexiest, most sensual human beings I know. Where is this self-doubt coming from? It's not like you!"

Rising to her feet, Mercedes began to wander restlessly around the small room. "I guess it's because I…haven't really had any sort of physical relations with a man since John."

Nicci's mouth fell open. "Oh, sis. That's been such a long time. Why? Don't you get lonely for a man's company?"

Her eyes full of sad shadows, Mercedes swallowed at the emotions thickening her throat. "I wouldn't let myself think about it. But when I met Gabe, everything just seemed to burst to life. And now I'm not even sure I know how to be a woman around him."

Picking Sara Rose up in her arms, Nicci walked over to Mercedes and cupped a gentle hand against the side of her face.

"You know how. Just be your beautiful self."

Be herself? She'd been an airman for so long that she'd almost forgotten that she was also a part of a family, a woman with basic desires and a heart that needed nurturing. It had been easier to focus on her job, where she could forget the shame and heartache she'd felt over John, push aside the second devastating mistake she'd made by trusting Drew. It had been convenient to let herself think that serving her country was all that she would ever need.

But now she was beginning to see that she wanted more. She wanted a family. Someone to love who would love her back. If that person was Gabe Trevino, she had to find the courage to show him. Even more, to trust him with her heart.

## *Chapter Seven*

The ratchet slipped, causing hunks of grease and dirt to fall on Gabe's face and join the sweat that was already there.

Muttering a curse under his breath, he refastened the tool to the oil plug, then grunted with relief as the threads gave way to his shove.

Dammit, he didn't have time to change the oil in his truck. Neither did he have time to wait around town for a mechanic, so he'd chosen the lesser of two evils.

With the plug finally out, the dirty crude began to drain into the flat plastic pan he'd positioned beneath the motor. While he waited for the motor to empty, he climbed from beneath the truck and unscrewed the cover on the brake fluid well.

Satisfied with the measurement, he was returning the cover when he heard a vehicle approaching behind him. Since he could count on one hand the number of visitors he'd had since he'd moved here three months ago, the sound was both totally unexpected and a tad irritating. He'd had a hell of a day already, and there wasn't much sunlight left. He didn't want to have to round up a drop light just to finish servicing the truck.

Reaching for the straw hat that he'd laid on the front fender, Gabe screwed it down on his head, then peered beneath the shade of the brim at the approaching truck. It was several years old and white. At first glance the driver was obscure, but as the vehicle grew nearer, he could see it was a woman.

Mercedes.

She'd warned him that she might show up at the line shack sometime, but a part of him believed she never would. Or maybe he'd hoped, more than believed. Either way, she was here. And now, in spite of his exhaustion, he was going to have to find the strength to keep her at arm's length.

Using the sleeve covering his forearm, he reached up and wiped at the grime covering his face. A few feet away, she parked her mother's old work truck and hopped to the ground with energy to spare.

Gabe walked over to greet her.

"I see you found your way out here," he said.

She smiled. "I've never forgotten it," she informed him, then glanced toward the raised hood of his truck. "Having problems?"

"No. Just servicing the engine."

She looked back to him. "You should have gotten one of the hands to do it for you."

"I like doing things for myself." Besides, he wanted the other ranch hands to think of him as an equal. Not as a higher-up who got special favors from the family. He'd rather be one of them than above them.

"I don't blame you for that."

She stepped closer and beneath his lowered lashes, Gabe allowed his gaze to travel over her long legs encased in faded blue jeans, the yellow shirt that clung to her midriff and made a low V between her breasts. It didn't matter that the clothes appeared to be well-worn work clothes or that her feet were covered in old cowboy boots with scuffed and scarred toes. She looked as sexy as hell.

"So this is the evening you decided to surprise me with a visit? Or are you here on business?" he asked.

She shook back her heavy hair, which was tied away from her face with a silk scarf a shade lighter than the pale yellow tresses.

"A little of both. I have some last-minute photos to show you. I couldn't find you at the ranch, so I decided to look for you here. But don't let me interrupt. I'm in no hurry and, besides, I'm pretty handy with a wrench—I can help."

She walked over and began poking and prodding at the engine, testing the belts and opening the radiator cap. "Have you checked the brake fluid and air filter? The transmission fluid?"

"I haven't gotten to all of those yet. But I can—"

She waved a dismissive hand at him. "Of course you can. But two can do it faster. You deal with the oil and I'll take care of everything up here," she told him.

Knowing it would be futile to keep arguing with her, Gabe slid under the truck and got back to work while Mercedes started removing the old air filter.

"Yeew. This thing looks awful," she exclaimed. "Got a new one anywhere?"

"In the tool box on the truck."

She went around to the back of the truck and Gabe tried to refocus his attention to the task at hand. It was difficult when he knew she would be back at any moment to stand near his head. She'd be stretching that long, curvy body under the hood to replace the filter and he'd have to imagine while his body grew harder and harder. Dammit.

"I didn't see you around the barn today," she said as she worked. "Did you take the day off?"

Gabe realized he should have called and told her that he'd be away from the ranch for the better part of the day. But he'd conveniently ignored the task. Interacting with her, in even the smallest way, unsettled him no end. Because he was beginning to like her. And that could only lead to problems.

"Sorry. I should have let you know. I've been riding all day with your brother and a couple more wranglers. One of the ranch's foundation stallions and a mare got out of a holding pen last night and took off for parts unknown. We finally found them this evening about four miles from the ranch yard."

"Oh, my. Did you get them corralled?"

He tossed the empty plastic jug into the back of the truck. "About a couple of hours ago."

"That's good. How did they get out? Someone left the gate open?"

He chuckled wryly. "No. It appears the stallion tore down a part of the fence. Or could be the mare wanted to get away from him and tore it down. It would be hard to say which one to pin the blame on."

"Maybe they both wanted out," Mercedes suggested with a grin. "Just to run and have fun."

That was probably right, Gabe thought ruefully. Whenever a male ran after a female, she always led him on quite a chase.

"No matter," he said. "We had a hell of time getting them captured again. Lex was saddle-weary. You didn't see him come in before you left the ranch?"

"No. Nicci came by my office and I was late getting away. I thought about waiting until morning to show you photos, but

I need to make the mail pickup before noon. If you decide I need to take different shots, I knew I'd need more time."

So she did really need to see him on business. He should have known she hadn't raced all the way out here just to see him. What in hell ever made him think she would? She could have her pick of wealthy, well-educated men. Men who mixed well with her social set. She'd never be seriously interested in a cowboy with horse manure on his boots. Besides, he didn't want her to be, he flatly reminded himself.

"Let me finish up here and I'll take a look," he said to her.

After motioning her out of the way, he started the engine to circulate the new oil, then after a couple of minutes shut it off and slammed the hood.

Mercedes looked at him with arched brows. "What about checking the transmission fluid? The engine has to be running for that. And have you greased all the sockets?"

She obviously understood mechanical workings and he admired her knowledge. Still, it irked him that she thought he needed instructions. Sherleen had always been quick to tell him how to do everything, as though he were ignorant or incapable of handling anything. After their divorce, he'd sworn to never get involved with another woman who told him what to do or how to do it.

"Don't worry. I'll take care of that later." Gabe gestured toward the house and the two of them began to walk in that direction. "Where did you learn about machinery?"

"From Dan, an old wrangler who worked on the ranch for probably sixty years or more. He was a hell of a cowboy, but he also knew how to keep things running. He maintained all the tractors and trucks, hay equipment, anything with wheels. I adored the old man and liked to hang around the ranch yard and help him. Mom and Dad never knew it, but he'd tell me shady stories about when he was young and all the escapades he'd had with the, uh, ladies. Anyway, he taught me a lot about motors and things. And maybe a little bit about fast women," she added with a laugh.

Amused, Gabe glanced at her. "What ever happened to this Dan? Is he still around?"

"He's in his nineties now and Nicci and Ridge keep a close watch on his health. Not to mention Cook. Dan's had a crush on her for years, but the most she'll give him is a pie or a box of homemade cookies."

"Poor man," he replied. "Sounds as if he only gets the crumbs."

"I wouldn't say that. That's more than Cook will give any other man."

"Oh? Is she a man hater or something?"

"No!" she said in a half-scolding tone. "Cook doesn't hate anyone. Her heart is too big for that. But she—well, she was widowed way back in the sixties. She'd only been married to her husband a short time when he went to Vietnam. I guess it's as if her love is still frozen in that time—still there with him."

"That's tragic."

"Yes. But on the other hand, she had something with him that some will never have in a lifetime. I think old Dan is wise enough to know that and accept it."

Even though she was talking about Cook, he could hear a dreamy bit of romance in her voice. After the other night at supper and the bitter story she'd told him about her broken relationship, he was surprised to hear the soft wistfulness in her words.

Not wanting to dwell on anything to do with hearts and flowers, Gabe said, "It sounds like the ranch has had some lifetime workers."

"Most people that come to work for us stay." Her glance at him was surreptitious. "Are you going to join the ranks of the stayers?"

Was she feeling him out for personal reasons or did she truly want to know how he felt about working and living on the ranch? Gabe told himself that, either way, he couldn't let it matter to him.

"So far, living here on the Sandbur is much better than going from town to town, place to place. I can see myself growing old here. But nothing in life is ever certain."

"Except death and taxes," she added, completing the old saying.

By now they'd reached the porch of the little house. Stepping onto the planks, Mercedes wrapped her arms around one of the fat cedar posts that supported the porch's roof and looked wistfully out at the lone pine shading the yard. In the years since she'd been gone, the tree had grown tremendously. Some of the branches now reached the roof of the house and each time the wind blew she could hear it whispering through the needles as they scratched against the corrugated iron. The sound was a part of nature's music, added to the bawl of a nearby calf, a horse's nicker, the high-pitched buzz of cicadas. She hadn't realized how much she'd missed those sounds until she'd returned to the Sandbur.

"My family expects me to stay here."

"But is that what you expect to do?" he asked.

Mercedes looked over her shoulder at him, wondering if any of that actually mattered to him. He'd made a decision to make his home here long before he'd ever met her. And she figured his decision to stay through the years ahead would not depend on the direction her own life took.

"That's my plan." She released her hold on the post and

looked around her. "The porch is longer than what I remembered. I guess Mother's had contractors out here building on. She can't leave anything simple," she added with a short laugh.

"She will now. I've told her I don't want anything else changed." Realizing he had little choice but to invite her inside, he gestured toward the door. "Would you like to come in?"

"Thanks. I'm dying to see the inside."

He opened the wooden screen door, then another oak door behind it. As they stepped into the cool living room, Mercedes said, "When I stayed out here, the only heating and cooling system was opening or closing the windows and doors. This is very modern. And the wood floor is beautiful."

"Geraldine insisted on putting in new flooring and appliances. But everything else is the same." He gestured toward an opening that led to the back part of the house. "The bathroom is still in the same place if you'd like to wash up before you look around."

She held up her greasy hands and laughed. "I'd better. Thanks."

Mercedes found her own way to the bathroom and shut the door behind her. As she scrubbed at the grease on her hands, she glanced around the small, but efficient space. There were no frilly decorations to play up the beige tiled walls, just white towels and washcloths, a blue plastic shower curtain and a blue rug on the floor. In front of her, below a small oval mirror, a single shelf held a razor, a shaving cup with soap and brush and a flat hairbrush. It was all neat, utilitarian and very masculine, like Gabe.

Moments later, she retraced her steps to the kitchen and found him washing his hands at a double, stainless steel sink.

Being alone with him was beginning to make her nerves

jump and jitter. How could she want the man, yet at the same time be frightened of wanting him? It was crazy.

At the sound of her footfalls, he glanced up. "Go ahead and look through the house, if you'd like. I'm going to change out of this dirty shirt."

"I'll wait for you to show me through it." Her smile was hesitant. "That way you can't accuse me of being snoopy like Lex always did back when we were kids and he'd let me come into his room. I'd pick up one thing and he'd start yelling. He always guarded his mementos with his very life."

He ripped off a length of paper towels and dried his hands. "Well, you don't have to worry about putting your hands on the wrong thing. I don't keep mementos."

"Why not?"

He darted an impatient glance her way. "I guess I'm just not the sentimental type, Mercedes."

She'd not thought of herself as being overly sentimental, either. But she supposed the memories lining her bedroom shelves said otherwise. "Hmm. I thought everybody kept little things from important moments in their lives."

"What I've kept, I wouldn't want anyone to see," he said brusquely, then stepped away from the sink and motioned for her to follow him.

Trying not to let his curtness get to her, she followed him into the living room. "You've already had a quick view of this area. There's not much here. I kept some pieces of the furniture that were already in the house and added a few of my own."

A couch and armchair done in navy leather faced the two long windows that looked over the front yard, which in all rights, couldn't be called a yard. The uneven ground was actually just pasture grass cropped short by cows.

"You don't have a television?"

He shook his head. "Don't have time for it. I keep a radio. And I read a bit at night. But most times I'm too tired for even that."

"I'm sure," she agreed knowingly. "Wrestling young horses around all day must physically wear on a person. But— well, Mother has made several comments lately that she thinks you do too much. She wants to hire more help for you."

He grimaced. "She needs to get that off her mind. I do things at my own pace. And the wranglers that help me are plenty enough. Your mother is sometimes too generous for her own good."

Mercedes walked over to where he stood near a small farm table with one chair pushed beneath it. Scattered across the top were several notebooks neatly stacked and an open accordion folder jammed with envelopes and other papers.

"Sometimes Mother can go overboard. But that's because she truly cares about people."

"Yeah," he agreed. "She's genuine."

He moved away from the table and she followed a step behind him as he headed down a tiny hallway where the bedrooms were located.

*Bedrooms.* Oh, dear, maybe she'd made a mistake in wanting to see the house, she thought. But it was a bit too late to be concerned about it now.

Hoping to talk away her nervousness, she said, "Yes, Mother is exactly the woman you see. She's also going on vacation. Her beau, Senator Wolfe Maddson, is taking her next week to his cabin up on the river at Concan. I think she already has four bags packed," she added with a little laugh. "No telling how many she'll have by the time she leaves."

He paused at the open doorway of the larger bedroom and Mercedes tried not to notice the broad expanse of his shoulders, the way his black hair curled against the back of his neck. He was the most sexual creature she'd ever seen in her life and the funny part of it was, he wasn't even trying to be.

She stifled a sigh.

He said, "You don't sound as if you resent her going."

"Why no," she said with a bit of dismay. "Why would I?"

He shrugged. "Because she has affections for a man other than your father."

Shaking her head, Mercedes said, "Mother has lived for a long time without companionship. More than anything, I want her to be happy." Her gaze settled on his face. "Wouldn't you want the same for your mother?"

His eyelids dropped to cover any feelings she might have spotted there.

"I can't answer that, Mercedes. I always saw my parents together and that's the only way I can imagine them."

Sensing that her question had called up bad memories for him, she tried to make amends. "If I could bring them back for you, Gabe, I would. But since I can't, I'll share my mother with you. She'd like that idea."

His gaze flickered to her face. "What makes you think I need a stand-in mom?"

The sudden need to reassure him had her placing a hand on his arm. "Everybody needs somebody."

He glanced down to where her hand rested on his arm and suddenly the air around them seemed to disappear, leaving Mercedes feeling so smothered that she was dizzy from lack of oxygen. Beads of sweat started trickling down her rib cage and between her breasts. The man affected her in ways he couldn't imagine. Or could he? Was he reading the wicked thoughts darting through her mind? Dear God, she prayed not.

"Uh, this is where I sleep," he said after a moment.

The quietly spoken words seemed to break the sparked atmosphere between them. Mercedes quickly jerked her hand from his arm and followed him across the threshold.

Like the rest of the house, it was sparsely furnished, yet she could see signs of him in the row of cowboy hats hanging from pegs along one wall. Most were battered and sweat-stained, telling Mercedes that he'd owned them for a long time.

The bed itself was a standard size with a scrolled iron head- and footboard. Presently the covers were tumbled to expose a set of white sheets. Mercedes tried her best not to imagine him lying there, his bare brown skin in stark contrast to the pristine cotton. Yet her imagination went on without her permission, and the sweat that had so far remained beneath her blouse began to bead across her upper lip.

Drawing in a deep breath, she forced her gaze away from the bed and over to a cane-bottom chair. Thrown over the back was a pair of fancy tooled chaps, the flashy, fringed sort that rough stock riders used on the rodeo circuit.

Walking over to them, she lightly fingered the oak leaf pattern decorating the belt. "Are these yours?"

"Yes," he said quietly. "I've not worn them in years, though."

She glanced curiously over her shoulder at him. "You used to ride broncs?"

He nodded. "Saddle broncs. For a while, when I was very young."

"Really? So did Lex," she told him. "But he got tired of the aches and pains that went with it."

His expression turned wry. "I got tired of being broke. And I decided I'd rather be training a horse not to buck than trying to ride one that did."

Turning away from the chaps, she leveled a teasing little

smile at him. "You fibbed to me a while ago, Gabe Trevino. You told me that you didn't keep mementos."

He frowned. "Those aren't a memento, they're a reminder."

"Of what?"

"Not to ever be that man again."

She simply stared at him and hoped he would elaborate. After several silent moments, she was about to decide he didn't want to share his personal past with her when he leaned a shoulder against the doorjamb and said, "After my parents died, my uncle raised me. A year before, his wife had left with their two boys and he was a bitter guy that liked to drown that bitterness in beer. But he was family and I needed a place to stay. And for the most part, he was good to me."

Something in his words pulled her toward him. "What about your other siblings? They didn't go to live with this same uncle?"

"At that time, my sisters were already married. My brother went to live with one of them. I stayed with Uncle Tony because I didn't want to leave Texas. Just to think of that prospect scared the hell out of me."

Empathy softened her voice. "Oh, Gabe."

Sardonic grooves marked his cheeks. "I was only eleven years old, but already strong-minded. Anyway, Tony wasn't too much on discipline or parenting. He pretty much let me run wild. After a while, I figured his indifference was because he didn't care about me. By the time I graduated high school, I wanted to get away. Any way. Anyhow. Riding broncs let me do that. And for a year or so, I traveled from one end of the country to the other, drinking, carousing, not ever thinking about tomorrow or the risks I was taking. Breaking my neck didn't worry me. I'd already lost everything anyway. Or so I believed."

"Something must have happened to change you," she stated.

"I got word that Tony was very ill. I raced straight back to Texas to help him—or at least try."

Mercedes was puzzled. "But I thought you left because you were at outs with your uncle?"

He shrugged. "He was my father's brother. To think of losing him, too, shook the ground right under me. It shook me even more when I got to the hospital. His kidneys and heart were barely functioning. Drinking doesn't mix with diabetes. Tony learned that the hard way."

"Did he recover?"

"After a long recuperation. I stuck around to help him and—"

Mercedes interrupted. "You mentioned that he had sons. Didn't they show up to help their father?"

Gabe snorted. "Belinda pretty much brainwashed the sons into thinking their father was the cause of their divorce. They abandoned him. After that, I became his son."

"At least you were there for him," Mercedes said, then looked at him thoughtfully. "How did you two make it financially? If he was ill and you'd given up your riding career to be with him, you must have had a struggle on your hands."

Straightening away from the doorjamb, he ran a hand around the back of his neck. "I put in long hours nailing shingles for a local roofing contractor. And when Tony's health began to return, he took in a few horses to train."

"You learned about horses from him?"

Even at a distance, she could see his eyes soften in a way she'd not seen before.

"Everything I know I owe to him."

The fact that he was so humble about his skills, so quick to give credit to others rather than himself, was one more thing Mercedes liked about the man.

"So how is your uncle now?"

A faint smile touched his lips. "He's healthy and sober, thank God. A few years ago, he moved away from Grulla and took a job up on the Four Sixes." His eyes met hers. "I don't get to see him as often as I'd like anymore. But time or distance could never change our relationship. We needed each other back then. We still do."

She glanced over her shoulder at the chaps lying across the back of the straight-back chair. He'd come a long way since those days, she thought. Financially and emotionally.

Suddenly moving past her, he walked over to the closet. "If you'll excuse me, I'll change out of these dirty clothes. Make yourself at home and help yourself to anything in the kitchen."

She thanked him, then shut the bedroom door behind her as she left the room. As she passed the open doorway of a second bedroom, she peeped inside to see that the room had been more or less turned into storage space.

The pine bed and dresser she remembered from years back were nowhere to be seen. Instead, there were several cardboard boxes filled with odds and ends and a couple of shelves lined with paperback books. A corner was piled with old cowboy boots and another with a fancy tooled trophy saddle resting on a wooden stand.

Intrigued by the saddle, Mercedes stepped into the room and over to the stand. The saddle's leather was still shiny from its coat of lacquer, telling her that it had never been ridden. The tooling was deep and done by hand, which would have made the cost of building the item skyrocket.

On both stirrup fenders, raised letters were stenciled. *San Antonio Cutting Championship 1996.* Had Gabe won the saddle? He'd said he didn't keep mementos, but she was discovering that wasn't entirely true. The chaps in his bedroom had proven that. They had also proven that in spite of the image he wanted to project, he was a family man at heart. He loved and needed as much as the next man. Maybe even more than the next man.

Touching the seat of the saddle, she wondered what had happened to end his marriage and wondered, too, if he would ever have the heart to try again.

## Chapter Eight

Five minutes later, when Gabe entered the kitchen, Mercedes was sitting at the kitchen table, sipping from a foam cup.

She smiled brightly at him.

"I made coffee. Would you like some?"

Before he could answer, she rose to her feet and poured it for him.

"Thank you," he said as he took the cup from her hand.

Her breathing shallow, her gaze quickly flicked over him. He'd changed into jeans and a long-sleeved blue checked shirt that was, in spite of the heat, buttoned at the wrist. Remembering the scars she'd spotted on his wrist that day at the horse barn, she began to wonder if the long sleeves were more than just a barrier to the hot, tropical sun. Perhaps the sleeves were hiding more scars than those she'd glimpsed.

Mercedes hated the idea that he might have endured that much physical trauma, especially when he'd had more than his share of emotional injuries in his life. But she wouldn't ask. Not this evening. He'd already opened up about his past much more than she'd ever expected, and for now that was enough to make her happy.

He looked at her over the rim of his cup. "So—where are the photos you needed for me to see?"

Was he that anxious for her to leave? Even though she told herself not to let it bother her, the idea hurt.

"I left them in the truck." She cast him an apologetic smile. "I'm sorry I'm disturbing your evening. It's just that it's been a long time since I've been out here. And I was thinking—before it gets completely dark, would you mind if I walked down to the river? Maybe you'd like to come with me?" she added, hoping she didn't sound overly eager for his company.

He scowled toward the window over the kitchen sink where one could catch a glimpse of the San Antonio as it meandered through a pair of steep banks.

"I don't have any business down at the river."

She rolled her eyes. "I don't, either. Don't you ever just do something for pure pleasure?"

Her question caused his gray gaze to slide slowly down her body, and Mercedes felt the small kitchen suddenly grow even smaller.

"I have my moments," he clipped, then gestured toward a back door. "Let's go. It'll be dark soon."

He was going, but he obviously didn't want to. Mercedes wanted to tell him he didn't have to do her any favors, but she kept the remark to herself as they stepped onto a screened-in back porch furnished with cushioned wicker furniture and several huge potted plants.

Seeing the surprise on her face, he explained, "Your mother

did this. Even though I told her I didn't have time to sit out here. Not working sixteen-hour days."

"No one expects you to put in that many hours."

"I do it because I want to. Isn't that why you went into the military? Because you wanted to?"

She'd gone into the military for a myriad of reasons, some of which she wasn't ready to share with him. She said, "I understand what you're saying."

The porch was built on the side of a hill, making the wooden steps descend steeply. Mercedes was surprised when his hand came around her upper arm to offer her a steadying brace.

Once they reached the sandy ground, there was a trail that led beneath a hackberry tree.

Thankfully, the setting sun had dropped the temperature to a bearable point. Above their heads, a brisk wind began to rattle the leaves.

Mercedes glanced up at the patch of sky visible between the tree branches. "Are we in for a rain shower?"

"I don't know, but it would sure be welcome."

Shaking back her hair, Mercedes sighed with a bit of pleasure. "The wind is nice."

Gabe realized he could now let loose her arm, but he didn't want to. It felt good to touch her, to feel the warmth of her flesh beneath his fingers.

Since the path was too narrow for them to walk comfortably abreast, he allowed Mercedes to walk on the smooth trail while he remained on the outer edge, where tufts of sage and nut grass forced him to watch his step. The fact that he was strolling along with her, for no real purpose except pleasure, felt odd, although he wasn't sure why. This wasn't the first time he'd been outdoors with a woman. He and Mercedes had shared that outdoor supper only a few days ago. Yet this felt entirely different. It was as if the two of them were setting off on an adventure together, and he was letting her lead him to new and secret places that he'd never seen or dreamed about. For the first time since he'd been a youngster, he felt the fun of the moment.

"What was the weather like over in Diego Garcia?" he asked as they carefully stepped their way forward.

"Tropical," she answered. "Hot and humid with lots of rain."

The trail suddenly reached the edge of the steep bank, where it spilled down the side, then wound through a stand of willows. Near the bottom, they stopped on a sandy bar and stared out at the sluggish water slowly working its way to the Gulf some thirty miles away.

"I don't know much about the military, but I thought Diego Garcia was a naval base. Weren't you in the Air Force?"

"I was and it is," she answered. "But a few Air Force people are there working in different capacities."

"Are military people the only ones living on the island?" he asked. She seemed so independent and strong-minded that it was hard for Gabe to imagine her in such a structured day-to-day routine, taking orders from superiors.

"Civilian contract workers are there."

She didn't offer more, and that surprised Gabe. Normally, she was eager to talk. Was there something about the place she wanted to forget?

In spite of his plans to keep an emotional distance from her, he wanted to know about her past, about the things that had affected her and eventually sent her back here to the Sandbur.

"So what was it like there?"

A heavy sigh slipped from her. "It wasn't any different than any other military base. I did my job and relaxed on my time off."

"You didn't have a boyfriend?"

Her features took on a bitter cast. "I didn't want one."

"Why not?"

From beneath her long dark lashes, she darted him an impatient glance. "Because I was more interested in my work. And since I worked with men, I learned it was best to keep things professional."

Gabe couldn't imagine any man in his right faculties standing next to this woman and not feeling some sort of spark. Just looking at her from a distance heated his blood. And somewhere in the undercurrent of her voice, he suspected she'd dealt with something or someone that she wanted to forget.

Secrets. It was obvious she had them and that she didn't want to share any of them with him. But that hardly surprised Gabe. He'd been married to a woman who'd made a profession out of keeping secrets from him. Sherleen had hidden everything from money to relationships from him. Then when he discovered them, she expected him to forgive and understand.

Dear God, he didn't want to dwell on that part of his life now. He didn't want to think that Mercedes could ever be on Sherleen's level. But how could he ever know without letting himself get close to her? And once that happened, it would be too late to protect himself if he was wrong about her.

"So where were you stationed before you went to the island?"

"After basic I was sent to Edwards in California, then on to Peterson in Colorado. That's where I furthered my training in intelligence. I didn't care for the cold and the snow, though, and asked to be transferred."

Before he could ask her anything about those places, her expression became totally shuttered. She moved away and began walking close to the river's edge. For a few moments, Gabe stared thoughtfully after her, then forced himself to rise and follow. A few feet beyond, an oak tree had grown at a severe slant out over the water. With the balance of a cat, Mercedes walked out on the huge trunk and sat down.

Gabe felt like an idiot as he carefully tread onto the tree to join her. He'd not behaved like this since he'd been a small kid. What was he doing following her around like this? He'd had a hell of a day. This was the last thing he needed. But once he sat down next to her, he had to admit it was a cozy seat with the twilight settling around them and the water running lazily beneath their dangling boots.

Mercedes's sigh was audible as she looked around her. "Now this is nice. Very nice."

She tossed him an impish grin and Gabe decided she must have pushed away whatever dark thoughts had been on her mind. He was glad. Dealing with her in a happy mood was much easier than imagining her brooding over a military man.

"I have to confess that this place caused me and my cousin Cordero a lot of problems. Instead of doing our chores, we'd sneak down here and go swimming. The last time we were caught, we were both grounded for a month. Because of that, I missed a party that my best friend was having. At the ripe old age of fourteen, I thought the world was coming to an end and I'd never survive."

"Obviously the grounding taught you a lesson," he said.

"No. A few weeks later, Cordero persuaded me to come out here and go for another dip. He was good at that. He could charm a snake if he tried."

"Sounds as if he was your partner in crime."

She laughed softly. "Yes, he was. I really miss him, you know. But if he's happy living over in Louisiana, that's what matters the most." She looked at him from the corner of her eye. "And if he were still here, then you probably wouldn't be."

Was she trying to say his coming here had affected her in

an important way? No. He couldn't start thinking that he could ever be important to this woman. She might want him, but she would never need him. Not the way a man wanted to be needed.

Shoving his straw hat back on his forehead, he wiped at the sweat with the back of his sleeve. "Everything happens for a reason."

She didn't say anything to that and after several long moments of silence passed, she gestured toward the river.

"See what you've been missing by not coming down here? It's beautiful."

It wasn't the river that made this place special, he thought. It was her. She made walking, talking, even breathing, extraordinary and that realization was beginning to nag him with worry. He didn't want anything becoming special to him. Even the horses that he trained, he tried to keep at an emotional distance. Attachments only caused heartaches. But his heart often got in the way of his plans to remain indifferent.

After more silence passed, she said, "I saw the trophy saddle in the spare bedroom. Did you win it?"

"Ten years ago."

"You don't ever ride it?"

"I want to keep it preserved. Uncle Tony talked me into entering a mare I'd been training in that particular cutting competition. I'd not expected to win, though, and it shocked me when I did. Needless to say, the saddle is significant to me."

Placing one hand on the small space of bark between them, she turned slightly to face him. "Why did winning surprise you? Didn't you think the mare was good enough?"

He chuckled with fond memory. "It wasn't her I was worried about, it was me."

Dimples marked the corners of her mouth and it was all Gabe could do to keep from leaning forward and pressing his lips to her cheeks, her lips. During the past days, he'd ordered himself to forget her. But their work threw them together, and every time they met, he was struck with proof that she wasn't a woman he could easily forget.

"All of us lack self-confidence at some time or another," she said lowly. "There were many times while I was going through basic training that I thought I couldn't make it. But somewhere, deep down, I found something to push me onward. Mainly, I didn't want to fail. And I didn't want to have to come home and tell Mother that I couldn't stand up to the pressure. She doesn't understand failure. She thinks her children, her niece and nephews should all be like this." She held up a tight, warrior-like fist. "But sometimes that's hard to do."

Each time the wind blew he caught the faint scent of jasmine coming from her skin and clothes. The fragrance stirred him almost as much as her nearness.

Gabe drew in a long breath and blew it out. "Yeah. We want to impress the people we love. And sometimes that's good. But sometimes it's the very wrong thing to do. I ought to know. I spent three years trying to impress Sherleen. But in the end, those were three years wasted. Three years that I should have spent being true to myself instead of trying to be something she wanted me to be. Hell, you can't expect to make anyone happy if you're not happy yourself."

Her blue eyes studied him for long, thoughtful moments. "Are you happy now?"

Was he? At times he could say he was content. He had a home that perfectly suited him. He had a job that was everything he'd ever wanted and more. Yet in the dark of night there were moments when he felt so completely and overwhelmingly alone. There were times he imagined children, his children, smiling up at him, holding their arms out to be hugged and loved by him. He thought of a woman in his arms, by his side. Supporting him. Growing old with him. But those were fleeting dreams. Mostly, he pushed them away and assured himself that he already had enough blessings to be a happy man.

"Why shouldn't I be?" he murmured the question. "I'm doing exactly what I want to do."

She shrugged and he could see she'd expected something more from him.

"That's about all anybody can ask for, isn't it?" she said softly.

The wistful note in her voice wound around his heart and spread a cold fog through his chest. He didn't like the feeling. It made him want to reach for her. To feel her warmth, to draw from it and then give the same pleasure back to her.

Suddenly a ball of emotion was choking him, forcing him to swallow. Next to him, Mercedes was nervously wiping her hands down the thighs of her jeans.

"Well, we'd better get to those photos," she suggested.

She was definitely right about that. They needed to leave this spot before he succumbed to the strange urges that were stirring inside of him.

Night was quickly closing in, intensifying the long shadows made by the tree limbs and other scrubby brush growing along the path. As they made their way back to the house, Gabe once again put a steadying hold around Mercedes's elbow.

As they reached the porch, Gabe blurted, "Have you eaten this evening?"

Surprise flickered across her face, yet Gabe figured she wasn't nearly as taken aback by his invitation as he was. The words had burst from him before he could even think of stopping them.

"Uh, no," she answered. "I came straight here after I left the office."

"Why don't you get the photos and I'll see what I can find for us to eat?" he suggested. "Do you need a flashlight to make it out to your truck, or can you see well enough without one?"

"I can see like a cat in the dark," she assured him. "I'll be back in two minutes."

Inside the kitchen, Gabe went to work pulling out an assortment of cold cuts, bread and condiments, and placing them on the small Formica table in one corner of the small room.

He was adding a bag of potato chips and two chilled soda cans to the rest of the food items when Mercedes returned, carrying a manila envelope.

She looked at the table and the things he'd laid out and her expression softened. "Gabe, I really should apologize for causing you this much trouble. But I won't. I love sandwiches!"

He gestured to the table. "Everything is ready."

She flashed him a smile. "Just let me wash up and I will be, too."

Minutes later, as Mercedes popped the last bite of a salami sandwich into her mouth, she couldn't think of a time that food had tasted any better than this. There was something very pleasurable about eating simple food with your hands and sharing a meal with the right person.

And slowly but surely, Mercedes was beginning to believe that Gabe was the right person. Being with him made her feel happy and alive. She didn't know where those feelings were going to lead her. If her past experiences with men were anything to go by, she was in for a brutal fall, yet she had no choice but to follow the whispers in her heart.

Once they'd eaten, Gabe cleared everything from the table

and Mercedes used the clean area to spread out the printouts of photos she'd taken.

As the two of them sat closely side by side, examining the snapshots, she tried to keep her mind on her business and off him.

"I tried to use the sunlight to emphasize favorable lines like long necks and high withers, but I'm not certain if I got the job done," she said with a hint of uncertainty. "When I told Mother I'd take on this job, she didn't tell me it would involve so much photography. I'm not a professional by any stretch of the imagination."

"I think all the photos are good, Mercedes. Very good."

She looked at him with relief. "Thanks. I was a bit worried you wouldn't like them."

"I'm not exactly in a position to fire you if I don't like them."

She frowned. "That's what you think. Mother would fire me in a minute if she thought you were disappointed with my work. Blood might be thicker than water, but not when it comes to the ranch work. But—" her gaze skittered shyly away from his face to settle on the photos "—that's not the point. I admire your work. And I want—well, I'd like for you to think I'm doing a good job, too."

"I do," he said simply.

She dared to look at his dark profile. "That makes me happy."

His gaze suddenly met hers and the dark fire Mercedes saw in his gray eyes shoved her pulse into overdrive.

"Mercedes, I've tried to tell you before that there's not much to like about me."

She tried to breathe, but her lungs felt smothered. The air around them was as charged and heavy as the atmosphere before a tornado. "Why don't you let me be my own judge?"

Disgust twisted his lips. "Because you're not seeing things—me—clearly."

Impulsively, she reached over and covered his hand with hers. "And I could be seeing more about you than even you can see about yourself. Did you ever think about that?"

The muscles in his throat worked as he swallowed, and in his eyes she could see dark doubts flicker. But those fleeting shadows were hardly enough to mask the simmering desire staring back at her, turning her insides into a bubbling cauldron.

"I think you're a stubborn little fool," he murmured.

Her head leaned a fraction closer to his. Close enough to see the pores in his brown skin, the creases at the corner of his eyes, the faint lines in the hard curve of his lips.

Oh, how she wanted to feel, to taste those lips again. The need burned so hotly inside her that it robbed her of breath. She could feel her heart thudding so madly against her ribs that it was causing her whole upper body to tremble.

"Why?" she whispered.

"For wanting to be next to me."

His hand lifted and his fingers threaded into the hair at her temple. The vein in her forehead throbbed beneath his touch and for once in her life, Mercedes was light-headed. If she didn't breathe or move soon, she was going to faint.

"And you won't be satisfied," he went on in a low, guttural tone, "until I want to be next to you."

Even if she was in any condition to speak, to try to deny his words would be futile. Since she'd met him at her coming home party, she'd made it clear in a thousand little ways that she was attracted to him. Now if she tried to turn away and pretend otherwise, it would be the same as lying to him and herself.

"What could be bad about that?" she finally managed to whisper.

"Just about every damned thing," he mouthed under his breath. "You sit there with your eyes full of sultry smiles, your lips calling to me. Yet you have no thoughts about tomorrow. Or what your game might do to us if—"

Mercedes wasn't about to let him go on. She didn't want him to rationalize, analyze or warn. Love couldn't flourish under those terms. It was as Nicci had said. Love couldn't be controlled.

Not wanting to give him the chance to protest more, she closed the tiny space between their faces and captured his lips with hers.

For the first few seconds, his mouth was frozen motionless, his body rigid and withdrawn. She was wondering if he was going to end the kiss as quickly as she'd started it, when he suddenly burst to life. His lips opened and the crush of his mouth upon hers swamped her with such overwhelming pleasure that all she could do was moan.

In a matter of moments, Gabe's arms were circling her shoulders, his lips deepening the kiss. The ability to think was lost for Mercedes. Behind her closed eyes, she gave herself up to the sensations erupting inside her head, the pleasurable ache that was building deep, deep inside her.

The moment Gabe's lips touched hers, he'd forgot all about the consequences of kissing the firebrand in his arms. At the moment, he didn't care what he'd find at the end of the road. All that mattered was the incredible sweetness of Mercedes's lips, the warmth of her body next to his, the need in her hands as they clenched the muscles of his shoulders.

He wanted her desperately. And right now he couldn't think of a good reason to stop.

Slowly, without breaking the contact of their lips, Gabe eased himself up from the chair while drawing her up with him. Once they were standing, he tugged her body forward until her breasts, hips, legs were all aligned with his.

The contact was like kerosene splashed on flame. Fire roared, then a slow, steady burn inched its way through his body until it finally settled in his loins. Instantly, his manhood hardened and in response, his hands slipped to her buttocks to pull her hips tight against the fiery ache bulging behind the fly of his jeans.

Breathless, he lifted his mouth away from hers to suck in long, ragged breaths.

While he restored his lungs, Mercedes's head fell limply back to expose the long, lovely line of her throat. Bending his head, he allowed his lips to glide down the soft skin until he reached the hollow near her collarbone. There he paused to draw in her jasmine scent, to collect on his tongue the sweat that had gathered in the shallow valley.

Goose bumps erupted along her skin, telling Gabe that his touch was affecting her in a way that thrilled him and urged him onward. Dropping his head even more, he looked for and found the point of one breast, then opened his mouth to bite softly through the layers of her blouse and bra.

Immediately her hips began to move against his in an age-old invitation that left no doubt to what she wanted.

"Oh. Oh, Gabe. Make—love to me," she pleaded breathlessly. "Please…make love—to me."

Whether it was the word she'd used or the fear of his own raging need that suddenly chilled him, Gabe didn't know. Either way, he released his hold on her and quickly stepped away, turning his back to her.

Behind him, Mercedes stared in dazed confusion at the rigid line of his shoulders. What had happened? One minute he'd been touching her as though there were no tomorrow and then he'd turn to a chunk of ice. "Gabe? What's wrong?" she whispered hoarsely.

"You."

The one word rattled around the room before he finally turned to look at her. She winced at the accusation in his gray eyes. How could he seem to want her and hate her at the same time? she wondered achingly.

"I want you to leave. Get out of here," he went on sharply. "Before both of us do something crazy. Something we could never fix."

Crazy? He thought it would be crazy to make love to her? The notion cut her so deeply that she couldn't have made any sort of reply even if she'd wanted to.

Instead of trying, she raced out of the kitchen and didn't stop until she'd reached her truck.

Back inside the house, Gabe glanced at the photos scattered across the table. But he didn't make a move to gather them up and intercept her before she drove away. He couldn't trust himself to face her again. Not tonight. Not when all he wanted to do was take her to his bed and forget there would ever be a tomorrow.

But tomorrow would come, he thought ruefully. He'd have to see her and the wanting would start all over again. And once again, he'd have to remind himself of all the reasons he couldn't let himself love her.

With a self-deprecating groan, he walked over to the table and began to stack the photos. Before he finished the task, he realized that rain was drumming loudly on the tin roof. Even so, the sound couldn't drown out the lonely beating of his heart.

## Chapter Nine

The next evening in Geraldine's bedroom, Mercedes stared at her mother in dismay. "Mother, you are kidding, aren't you?"

Geraldine didn't pause a beat as she placed a folded blouse in the suitcase lying open on the bed. Early in the morning, she was driving up to San Antonio to meet her beau, and from there the couple were driving to West Texas for a week. Mercedes had been aware of her mother's plans for days now. But she'd not been aware that Geraldine had also been making plans for Mercedes to accompany Gabe on a horse-auction trip that weekend.

"Mercedes, the Western Heritage Auction is not anything to kid about. It's not like going to the county sale barn where a few grade horses are run in the ring behind the cattle and the hogs. There will be buyers dressed in designer suits and handmade boots, horses that will sell for six figures. It's an important auction for buyers and sellers across the Southwest and beyond. You need to be there to get a sense of the sort of marketing ideas the Sandbur needs to focus on. And as a member of the Sandbur family, you should also be there to help Gabe represent our horses. It's that simple."

It was all Mercedes could do to keep from telling her mother in no uncertain terms that Gabe didn't want or need her help. But that would only arouse Geraldine's suspicions. Besides that, only three weeks had passed since Mercedes had agreed to take on the marketing job for the ranch. To start whining about her responsibilities now would make her look worse than difficult and ungrateful.

"I see," Mercedes said in a low, thoughtful voice. "I didn't realize the Western Heritage Auction was such a big deal."

"Very big," Geraldine replied matter-of-factly. She straightened from her bent position over the suitcase and leveled a direct gaze on her daughter. "Are you having a problem with this plan, Mercedes?"

Problem? Gabe had been so upset with her that he'd ordered her out of his house. And this morning, when she'd entered her office, she'd found the photos on her desk. He'd obviously placed them there early, so he wouldn't have to face her. Yeah, there was a huge problem, she thought dismally.

"No. I—um—I'm just—surprised to hear I'll be making the trip. I figured Lex would be a much better person than me to tag along with Gabe. They get on well together, and he's got more experience representing the Sandbur."

Shaking her head, Geraldine walked over to a long oak dresser and picked up a bag full of toiletries. "Lex is a cattleman. And that's where his expertise is needed most. Anyway, he's going to Florida this weekend—on business."

Fighting off a groan, Mercedes stepped to the foot of the bed and wrapped her hands around the carved oak post.

"Yes, I've heard about Lex's little trips to Florida. He says they're business, but who calls fishing and swimming and lounging around on the beach, business?"

Geraldine created a spot for the toiletries among the other things in the travel bag, then zipped the whole thing closed. "Lex has latched on to one of the best cattle buyers we have," Geraldine told her, "and if keeping the man happy includes beach recreation, then more power to your brother."

Mercedes frowned. "I wasn't complaining, Mother. I just think it's amusing that you call these trips of his to Florida business trips."

"But they are business trips," Geraldine countered. "It's not always pleasant cozying up to someone you don't know all that well." She placed the bag on the floor, then glanced skeptically at her daughter. "Are you having problems with Gabe? You don't sound exactly thrilled about this trip. If something is going on between you two that I need to know about, then you'd better let me in on it now. I'll be leaving the house at five in the morning."

This was the first time in years that Geraldine was going on a vacation and Mercedes wanted her mother's time with Wolfe to be quiet and special, without her having any nagging worries about her children or the ranch. Besides that, Mercedes would bite off her tongue before she'd admit to her mother that she'd thrown herself at Gabe and he'd rejected her. The whole thing was simply too humiliating.

"There's no problem. Don't worry." Mercedes straightened away from the footboard. "Does Gabe know that I'm going with him?"

Geraldine smiled, and if Mercedes hadn't known better, she would have sworn she saw a mischievous twinkle in her mother's eyes.

"I thought I'd let you tell him," she said.

Mercedes exhaled slowly. After last night, she was embarrassed to even face the man, much less inform him that the two of them would be making a five-hundred-mile trip together, and spend two nights sharing cramped quarters.

How was he going to take this news? *How do you think, Mercedes?* a sarcastic voice inside her answered. *The man literally ordered you to get away from him.*

Okay. So Gabe had ordered her out, she mentally argued with herself. But not before he'd ravished her with his lips, heated her body to the bursting point. He'd wanted her. Oh, yes, in spite of his sharp demand for her to leave, Mercedes had felt his desire. He couldn't be as indifferent as he wanted her to believe.

"I'll discuss the trip with him in the morning," Mercedes told her mother. Before Geraldine could say more on the subject, Mercedes quickly switched gears. "Are you sure you have everything ready for your own trip?"

Laughing, Geraldine looked over at the group of leather bags waiting to be loaded in her car. "Doesn't it look like I have everything?" Concern suddenly marked her face. "I hope you and Lex and Nicci don't resent me going with Wolfe for the next week or so to his summer cabin. Do you?"

"Not in the least. We want you to be happy, Mother. And you deserve this time away from the ranch. God knows how hard you work to keep this place going."

"I don't do any more than anyone else," she said dismissively. Then, in an uncharacteristic display of uncertainty, Geraldine's gaze dropped to the floor. "But the ranch isn't what I'm thinking of now, honey. It's you and Lex and the memory of your father that worries me. I know how much you both loved him."

Sensing that words weren't enough to ease her mother's mind, Mercedes walked over to Geraldine and wrapped her arms around her slender shoulders.

"We did love Daddy. But we also want you to be happy, Mother. And if Wolfe makes you happy, we're not about to stand in your way."

A wan smile touched Geraldine's lips. "I would expect that from you, Mercedes. But Lex—I'm not so sure. He was so very close to Paul. And being a man, I'm not sure he understands the loneliness a woman can feel when her spouse is gone."

Frowning, Mercedes asked, "Lex hasn't voiced any sort of disapproval about you dating Wolfe, has he?"

"No. But you know your brother. He's all jokes and laughs. Who knows what's really going on in that head of his."

Mercedes smoothed a hand over her mother's silver hair. "Trust me, Mother. You needn't be worrying about Lex. When it comes down to the bottom line, he loves you and wants you to be happy."

Sighing, the older woman turned away and crossed to the closet. "All right. I'll put that out of my mind. Now what about you? Can you handle this trip with Gabe?"

Mercedes couldn't handle Gabe in any way. He was a man with his own ideas about himself, her and life in general. If last night was any indication, he wasn't about to let her seduce him. And as for him seducing her, well, he'd already done that without even trying.

"I'll be fine, Mother. For the past eight years I've worked with men. Gabe isn't any different."

The words were hardly out of Mercedes's mouth, when that sarcastic voice inside her head was sounding off again.

*Liar, liar, pants on fire. Everything about Gabe is different. Everything you feel about Gabe is different.*

* * *

The next morning, Mercedes rose early enough to wave her mother off and make a pot of coffee before Cook arrived to make breakfast.

While she was eating an omelet and toast, Lex, dressed in starched jeans and shirt and brown ostrich boots, entered the kitchen. His streaked blond hair was slicked back from his face and he whistled beneath his breath as he headed straight to the coffeepot on the cabinet counter.

"Oh, what a lovely mornin' it is when I wake up to see two roses like this," he said, encompassing both Cook and Mercedes with his compliment.

From her position in front of the gas range, Cook snorted cynically as Lex kissed her cheek.

"What are you wantin' this mornin'? Hotcakes? Well, I'm not fixin' them, so don't bother askin'," she told him. "You can eat what your sister is eatin' and be thankful for it."

"My Lord, but you're crabby this mornin'. Why are you sticking your claws out at me? All I've ever done is love you," he told the older woman.

She looked at him with pursed red lips. "Well, to put it plainly, I'm feelin' pretty useless around here. First your mama leaves, now you and then Mercedes. I don't guess I need to even show up for the next few days, unless I want to help Jorge cook for the boys down at the bunkhouse. And he don't really need me."

Looking over her shoulder, Mercedes suggested, "Why don't you just enjoy the next few days? Relax. Go shopping."

Muttering under her breath, Cook began to break eggs into a glass bowl. "Why would I want to go shopping? I already have everything I need right here."

"Well, you could buy a new dress and surprise old Dan with a visit."

Cook let out a comical wail. "Me showing up would surprise the old codger, all right. Probably give him a heart attack."

Laughing, Lex curled his arm around the back of Cook's waist. "Are you telling me that your legs still look that good?"

Lifting the metal spatula from the stove top, she threatened to swat him. "Get away from here. Now! Or you're gonna be cookin' your own breakfast," she warned.

To show the old woman how worried he was, he kissed her on the cheek again, then sauntered over to his sister and eased down on the long bench across from her.

"So what's this about you leaving?" he asked as he sipped from his coffee mug.

"I'm going to be accompanying Gabe up to the Western Heritage Auction in Oklahoma City."

"Oh. That sounds like fun. Buying or selling?"

Mercedes's brows lifted in surprise. "I'm not sure about the buying. I know we're selling five."

Lex chuckled. "Just wait 'til you get up there, sis. You'll be buying, that's for sure."

She dropped her gaze from his face and refocused it on her plate. "It's not my place to be spending the ranch's money."

"Why not? You're just as much a part of this ranch as anyone else."

She gave her brother a halfhearted grin. "I've been gone for a long time. Let me pay some dues before I start buying livestock."

He patted her cheek, then glanced toward the swinging doors that led in and out of the kitchen. "Mom already gone?"

"She drove away before five o'clock."

"I haven't seen her this excited about anything in a long time." He turned a thoughtful look at Mercedes. "Do you think she plans to marry the senator?"

Mercedes shrugged. "I don't know. She's not mentioned that word around me. But it wouldn't surprise me. She wouldn't just go off with a man unless she really felt deeply for him."

Lex blew out a breath. "Yeah. That's what I was thinking."

Mercedes studied him for a moment. "Mother worries that you disapprove of her relationship with Wolfe. I told her you weren't that selfish."

Lex looked surprised. "Why would she think I'd disapprove?"

"Because you were so close to Daddy."

Rarely did Mercedes ever spot a serious look on her brother's face, but she was seeing one now.

"I'd give both my arms, anything, to have him back," Lex said. "But that has nothing to do with Mom finding happiness. She can't live in the past forever."

"Then you don't resent her relationship with Wolfe?"

"Hell no." He tapped a finger against the middle of his chest. "But if he or any man ever hurts her, he'll have me to answer to."

A knight in shining armor, she thought wryly. If only her gallant brother had been around to save her when John had broken her heart. But she'd been far away in Austin and he'd been here on the ranch, throwing his shoulders into being a cattleman with a mission. And she'd not wanted to share with Lex the humiliating mistakes she'd made with Drew. She'd always wanted her brother's admiration. She couldn't let him know, even to this day, that she'd let a playboy professor and a deceitful airman turn her head.

Lex's eyes sparked with sudden mischief. "So you're going with Gabe this weekend. How's he taking the news?"

A smirk twisted her lips. "He doesn't know about it—yet. I plan to tell him right after I finish breakfast."

"Hmm. I wouldn't want to be around when he hears you're tagging along."

The smirk on Mercedes's face shifted to a frown. "Why? You make it sound as if I'm a case of the measles, or worse."

"I figure Gabe considers women worse than measles."

*That's what you think,* Mercedes silently retorted. When his lips had fastened over hers, when his hands had cupped her breasts and his hips had ground into hers, it sure as heck hadn't felt as if he was treating her as though she had the measles. But that had been pure sex on his part, she reminded herself. Those moments she'd been crushed up against him had nothing to do with liking or loving. That part had come when the kiss had ended and he'd ordered her to get away from him.

"Well, he's gonna have to either like my company or ignore it," Mercedes said with far more confidence than she felt. "Because one way or the other, I'm going to go and do my job."

Some thirty minutes later, fingers of sunlight had already spread their hold across the ranch and crept up the sides of the barn. As Mercedes made her way to Gabe's office, the blustery words she mouthed to her brother cowered somewhere behind the nervous beat of her heart. So much for Nicci's sage advice, she thought ruefully. She'd tried her rusty sexuality on the man and he'd found it lacking. So where did that leave her plan to impress him?

At Gabe's office, she caught the sound of male conversation drifting from the open door. Deciding it would be best to leave and come back later, she turned to walk away.

"Mercedes," Gabe called out, "come in."

Realizing he must have spotted her, she stepped inside the small room with plans to tell him she'd come back later. But before she could acknowledge Gabe, her gaze caught sight of her uncle Mingo relaxing on the couch.

With a little cry of pleasure, she raced over to the older man and hugged him close. Mingo was more like a father to Mercedes than an uncle, and seeing him this morning was just the thing she needed to give her the courage to deal with Gabe.

"My, my, don't you look as fresh as a spring bluebonnet," Mingo declared as he gave his niece a tight hug.

"And you look like an old teddy bear," she teased, then tugged on the short bristle of white and black whiskers sprouting from his chin and upper lip. "When did you decide to grow this? Don't you know that facial hair makes a man look older?"

Clearly amused, he said, "If that's the case, then why do all the women I know seem to like it?"

Laughing with delight, she leaned close and rubbed her cheek against his chin in a testing way. "Aww, well, I guess it does feel nice. But it makes you look too autocratic."

Mingo laughed. "If I knew what that meant, I might do something about it."

Laughing with him, Mercedes explained, "It means you look as if you should be sitting on a throne with a scepter in your hand."

Mingo glanced over at Gabe and winked. "Just give me a bullwhip. That'll do me."

Mercedes kissed her uncle's cheek, then forced herself to face Gabe. He was watching her through narrowed eyes, as though her unexpected presence in his office was annoying. She tried not to let him get to her, but it was hard to do when just looking at the man sent odd little thrills straight through her. Had she really kissed those stern lips? In the light of day, it seemed impossible.

"Sorry to interrupt," she said to him, then glanced adoringly at Mingo. "But I don't often get the chance to see my uncle."

Mingo gave her an affectionate grin. "A beautiful young

thing like you shouldn't be wasting time with an old man like me anyway."

She frowned at him. "You're not old, Uncle," she scolded gently. "You're just reaching your prime." She looked pointedly at Gabe. "Did you know that my uncle is a living miracle? Three years ago, he couldn't walk or talk. He was in a nursing home— and sitting in a wheelchair instead of a saddle. Now look at him. He has to carry around a stick to knock the women away."

Close to her side, Mingo chuckled. "You're stretching that last bit about the women, aren't you, girl?"

She gave her uncle a sidelong glance. "Not from the stories Cordero tells me. He said Juan quit answering the phone because it was always some lady wanting to speak with you."

Mingo only slapped his knee and shook his head. Across from them, Gabe said, "I knew that Mingo had been disabled sometime back. I didn't know it was to that extent."

Mercedes nodded. "That's why I call him a living miracle. He was in Goliad late one evening when two thugs jumped him with a baseball bat and left him with a brain injury. Thankfully, a wonderful neurosurgeon over in Houston fixed everything back the way it should be, but Uncle Mingo still went through months of difficult therapy."

"Yeah," Mingo echoed. "Now the only thing left is to find the two hoodlums and put them behind bars."

Clearly surprised, Gabe's gaze vacillated between Mingo and Mercedes. "You mean, the persons that did this haven't been caught or prosecuted?"

Mercedes shook her head while Mingo said, "Sheriff Travers and the whole department are still working on the case. And I have faith, Gabe. I'll have my justice in due time."

The older man rose to his feet and announced he had to be going. "Gracia has her eye on a new horse up at San Marcos.

Matt says he'll buy the animal for her if I go have a look at him first." He chuckled fondly. "She's probably already sitting in the truck, waiting for her grandfather to show up."

"Have a safe trip, Uncle," Mercedes called after him. Once he was out of sight, she turned to Gabe. "I didn't expect you to have company this early in the morning."

His gaze was like a gray laser cutting hot streaks across her face and down the length of her body. "Mingo comes by fairly often," he drawled. "He likes to get updates on the horses. And I like to get his advice. He's already forgotten more things about horses than I've ever learned."

In spite of her nervousness, she warmed to him. How could she not, when he had nothing but kind words for her family? "I'm glad you don't resent him."

"Resent him, hell," he mouthed under his breath. "I don't have an ego problem, Mercedes. I'm not some jerk who thinks he's the only man alive that knows how to handle a horse."

Her pulse fluttered. "I never thought you were. And actually—I'm not here to discuss my uncle. I—"

"Mercedes, if you're here to discuss last night, then forget it," he said sharply. "I have."

Had he? That wasn't what the slumbering shadows in his eyes told her. But now wasn't the time to discuss their hot embrace in his kitchen. She had to get through this coming weekend without making a fool of herself.

"I assure you," she said stiffly, "that I have no intention of discussing that—lapse between us. I'm here about the upcoming auction."

His brows drew together to form a black streak above his gray eyes. "The Western Heritage Auction? What's that got to do with you? I thought all the pertinent information had already been sent. If not, it's far too late to be in the sale catalog."

Drawing in a bracing breath, Mercedes shook her head. "It's not about catalog information. I— Mother discussed the whole thing with me last night. She insists that I make the trip with you."

Silence ensued as Gabe stared at her. "No. I'm not about to take you on this trip."

His blunt refusal should have angered her. After all, she was a part of this ranch, too. She had as much right and reason to make the trip as he did. But as she studied his narrowed eyes and rock-hard jaw, all she could feel was hurt. Hurt that he obviously couldn't bear to think of spending that much time in her company.

*Oh, Mercedes, you've learned that things are bad when a man has the power to hurt you.*

"I'm sorry you feel that way, because Mother didn't leave either one of us a choice," she told him. "She wants me there to observe, to represent the Sandbur and to help you in any way you might need."

Rising to his feet, he walked over to a small table holding a coffee machine. "Then I'll talk to her," he said brusquely. "I'll tell her that I can handle things by myself."

"Too late. She left this morning to meet Senator Maddson in San Antonio. I have her cell-phone number if you'd like to call her. But I can tell you right now that arguing with her about this isn't going to make her happy. And I wouldn't like that at all. This is the first time in years that my mother's actually taken a vacation. I don't want her fretting—about anything."

Glancing over his shoulder, he stabbed her with an accusing gaze. "You're getting pleasure out of this, aren't you?"

Unable to remain still, Mercedes left the couch and walked over to the front of his desk.

"If you think I could possibly get pleasure from having someone tell me they don't want me around, then you've got to be crazy." She folded her arms against her breasts as she tried to hang on to her temper. "I argued with Mother about me making the trip. I told her that I didn't want to go because I knew you were going to react this way!"

Plopping his coffee back down on the table, he stalked over to where she was standing. "Of course you knew I would react this way, because you know as well as I do that the two of us can't be together! When we're together, we both act like fools!"

She drew in a long, shuddering breath. "Thank you, Gabe," she said with sarcasm. "I've always wanted a man to call me a fool."

He inched close enough for her to catch a whiff of the scents of soap and horses emanating from his denim shirt, to see the dark glint in his gray eyes and the moist sheen on his bottom lip. Even in anger, she was astonished at how much she wanted him.

"I included myself under that description." Shaking his head, he muttered a curse under his breath. "What in hell was Geraldine thinking?"

Her blood simmering, Mercedes tossed her head, sending her thick blond hair rippling down her back. "She was thinking that we're two adults with a job to do. She was thinking we're going to Oklahoma to do those jobs. Not to claw and hiss at each other."

His eyelids lowered as his gaze settled on her lips. "Or to make love," he whispered hoarsely.

*Make love.*

She didn't know whether it was those two words or the low growl in his voice that sent a sultry shiver down her spine. Either way, she couldn't stop her body from gravitating toward his. It was crazy, she thought. How could she still want this man so much even when he was making it clear he didn't want her around. "That—won't be on the agenda. Unless you want it to be."

His nostrils flared with disdain. "That won't be an option. Ever."

The sharpness of his voice brought a stinging ache to her throat. "Then that's the way it will be," she murmured.

Mercedes blinked hot moisture from her eyes and quickly turned to leave the office. She'd taken one step when his hand wrapped around her upper arm. Her heart racing from his unexpected touch, she dared to glance back at him.

"Was there something else?" she asked coldly.

His gaze flicked over her face in a dismissive way. "I'll be leaving the ranch yard at five in the morning. If you're not there on time, I'll leave without you. Got it?"

He knew that she was an early riser. For him to imply that she was some spoiled princess that didn't rise from bed until midmorning made her want to slap his face.

"Don't think for one minute I'll let you off that easily, Mr. Trevino. I'll see you in the morning," she muttered furiously. Jerking her arm free from his grasp, she rushed out of the office and didn't stop until she was halfway across the huge ranch yard.

By then, tears were on her face and she dashed them back with an angry hand. Eight years ago, she'd cried a bucket of tears over John. She'd learned a painful lesson about lying men, but apparently the lesson hadn't been enough. Drew had come along and once again she'd fallen into the trap. Now she was making that same mistake all over again with Gabe Trevino. But this time, she'd stay strong. She would stiffen her spine and show him that she wasn't going to let him walk all over her heart.

## Chapter Ten

Dark gray shadows still shrouded the ranch yard the next morning when Mercedes walked to the waiting truck and trailer parked near the horse barn.

Even though it was several minutes before five o'clock, the diesel motor was already idling and the cargo lights were on, along with the rows of lights illuminating the outline of the thirty-foot horse van. Five heads, their eyes goggled with safety screens, hung out the open windows, telling Mercedes the horses were all loaded and ready to travel.

She quickly stowed her bags in the living quarters of the trailer, then stepped out to see Gabe standing near the back of the big rig, apparently checking the van one last time to ensure the horses' care and well-being during the trip.

Mercedes didn't bother announcing her presence. Instead, she simply climbed into the cab of the freighter and waited for Gabe to join her.

Five minutes passed before the cab door finally opened and he climbed in the seat behind the wheel. By then, she'd already fastened her safety belt and tuned the radio to a station that played only Elvis. After all, she didn't intend to let Gabe dictate everything about this trip.

"Good morning," she greeted, forcing a normalcy to her voice that she was far from feeling.

He nodded slightly in her direction. "Good morning."

"Are we ready to go?" she asked.

He reached for the gearshift in the middle of the floor. "We're off."

In spite of their sharp exchange yesterday morning, Mercedes couldn't help but feel a spurt of adventure and excitement as the big truck began to lumber across the ranch yard, then on past the ranch's entrance.

The last time Mercedes had taken a major driving trip was back as a teenager. She'd gone with her uncle Mingo to Clovis, New Mexico, for a three-day horse sale. If this trip gave her only a fraction of the fun she'd had on that one, then it was something to look forward to. And maybe she could enjoy these days ahead, she thought hopefully. All she had to do was stay out of Gabe's way.

But how could she do that, when everything inside her wanted to be near the man?

After an hour's travel, the sun had risen high in the morning sky, and Gabe had directed the big rig onto a major interstate directly north through the heart of Texas. For the most part, his passenger had spoken very little. Whenever she did, it was only to make a comment about things she spotted along the highway.

Gabe had to admit he didn't know what to make of her quietness. Up to this morning, the Mercedes he knew normally chattered. But for the past hundred miles, she hadn't appeared interested in conversation or in him. Which was well and good, he thought sourly. He'd not wanted her on this trip in the first place. A man could take just so much temptation before he succumbed.

Still, he couldn't ignore the beautiful picture she made sitting only inches away from him, her face quiet and thoughtful as she gazed out at the passing landscape.

She'd dressed totally western for the trip in a red flowered shirt with white piping and wide cuffs buttoned at her wrist. The hems of her blue jeans were tucked into a pair of tall, black, cowboy boots, while the waist was cinched with a matching black belt. Her long hair was brushed in loose waves and pinned behind one ear with a silver tooled barrette.

She managed to look cute and classy at the same time and he wondered what her fellow airmen would think if they could see her like this. Had any of them known there'd been a cowgirl inside the military woman?

Or was she still a military woman inside that cowgirl outfit? It was a question that nagged Gabe daily. From the first moment he'd met her at the homecoming party, he'd formed the impression that she was a violet among a bunch of tough weeds. She didn't fit with the life of an isolated ranch, even one as big and wealthy as the Sandbur. He feared she was going through the motions of this marketing job just to appease her mother and the rest of the family until she found a job that would take her away again.

Either way, it couldn't matter to him, he told himself. Mercedes was off-limits.

Yeah, off-limits. In spite of all the times he'd told himself just that, in spite of the fuss he'd made yesterday about her coming on this trip, he couldn't stop the thrill he felt at having her near. It was stupid and dangerous. It went against every vow he'd made about letting a woman make him vulnerable again. But he couldn't help himself.

She began to shift in the seat and he glanced over in time to see her crossing her long legs and smoothing a hand down her shapely thigh.

"Are you getting tired?" he asked.

Faint surprise marked her face as she darted a glance at him. "No."

"Well, if you need to stop for the restroom or anything, just tell me. I'm not like those drivers who think they have to keep barreling on until they reach their destination."

Her brows piqued with interest. "That's hard to believe. To me, you've always come across as a man on a mission."

Why did he want to reach over and touch her? he wondered. Why did he want to drag his fingers down her honey-brown cheek, along the tender curve of her throat? Why did he want to believe the kisses she'd given him at the line shack had been more than fun and games?

"We're on a trip, Mercedes," he pointed out dryly. "Not a death march."

She straightened upright in the wide leather seat and stared at the windshield in front of her. "That's good to know," she said with a hint of sarcasm. "Especially after you so *kindly* accepted my part in this jaunt."

He groaned. "We're not going to go over that again, Mercedes. You're here. I'm here. We don't need to spend the next few days being hostile to each other."

Her head twisted toward him and as he watched her features soften into a beautiful smile, he felt his heart jerk, then begin to melt like a roasting marshmallow.

"That's the way I see it, too," she agreed. "And since you're being so agreeable for the moment, I should mention that Cook packed us a picnic basket. I thought we might stop at a roadside park for lunch."

She'd planned a picnic? That kind of lighthearted meal wasn't the sort of thing he normally shared with a woman. Partly because it had a family feel to it, and partly because the majority of his lady friends expected to be fed in nice restaurants. "Are you sure you'd rather not eat in a restaurant?"

Over the crooning voice of the King coming from the radio, he could hear her soft, impatient sigh. "It's always nicer to eat outside in the peace and quiet. Besides that, you could stop at every food joint from here to the Oklahoma border and not find anything as good as what Cook sent."

He might as well face it, Gabe thought, the woman was never going to be predictable. And he could only wonder what to expect from her next.

Three hours later, just outside the busy outskirts of Fort Worth, Mercedes spotted a roadside park with a wide, circular pull-off, plenty of grassy grounds and cement tables shaded by massive oak trees. Both agreed it would be a good place for lunch before they reached the hectic city traffic.

Gabe parked the rig in a far, out-of-the-way space, and Mercedes fetched the picnic basket from the front of the trailer. While she spread the food on a table located at one end of the little park, Gabe went to check on the horses and offer them a drink of water.

The day was hot and windy enough to toss Mercedes's blond hair all about her head. She was tying it back with a scarf when Gabe finally joined her. Thankfully, after their fragile truce this morning, he'd actually been easy to travel

the owner could be healed, too. When a person learns to focus their interest and affection on an animal, rather than himself, it changes him for the better. In the end, that gave my job some meaning. And isn't that what we all want—for what we do to have meaning?"

Mercedes absently stirred her plastic fork through the shredded cabbage. "Mmm. Yes. That's why I didn't want Mother fabricating a job for me. I couldn't stand that. It would be like living a waste."

Feeling his eyes upon her, she glanced up to see he was studying her with a skeptical expression.

"Lex has told me that you were very good at your job in the Air Force. He says you could easily get a nice position with the CIA, FBI or other government agencies. Do you ever think about that?"

She sighed. "It's an option. But I've spent years serving my country. After I was home at the Sandbur for a few days, I realized the ranch was my calling."

"Isn't that too convenient?"

Any other time, his question would probably have angered her, but something on his face told her that he wasn't being sarcastic; he actually wanted to know how she felt. That idea was enough to send a warm feeling spilling through her.

"It probably looks that way," she agreed. "But you see, my roots are important to me, too. The Sandbur isn't just a ranch that raises cattle and horses. It's a history. It's a family legacy—my family. My great-grandparents struggled through the Depression to hold on to the land. Their descendants before them carved the place out of the wilds, fought with outlaws and comancheros, only to have the homestead burned to the ground and their stock scattered by Santa Anna's army. But they never gave up on the ranch." She paused long enough to shake her head. "They all, including my own parents, have sacrificed so much to make the Sandbur what it is today. Surely you can see it's important for me to contribute my part?"

But why? Gabe wondered. Out of love for what she was doing or guilt that she'd spent the past years away from the ranch? If she'd only taken the job out of a sense of obligation, then would that be enough to make her stay?

"You knew all of this before you joined the Air Force. If you felt that passionately about the ranch, why did you leave in the first place?"

Her head dipped and hid the expression in her eyes as though his question made her ashamed. Gabe found himself wanting to reach across the table, to lift her chin and assure her that washing her with guilt had never been his intention. All he wanted was to dig inside her, to take out her feelings and see if they were actually coming from her heart.

"You're right. Eight years ago, I wasn't blind to the sacrifices my family had made for the ranch. But I—" Sighing heavily, she looked up, regret written on her face. "I had other issues going on at that time. I needed to get away—to get my life back in order before I could ever make a worthwhile contribution to anyone—especially my family."

Those other "issues" could only refer to the man who'd broken her heart, Gabe thought grimly. She'd said she was long over the guy, but that didn't ring true with him. If her heart was truly mended, she would've already found another man to love and marry. Yet she'd told Gabe with her own lips that she wasn't looking for marriage. The whole thing made him wonder if there was more to her reluctance to become a wife.

*Hell, it doesn't matter why she's chosen to stay single,* he told himself. He wasn't looking for a wife. And even if he were, Mercedes wouldn't be on his shopping list.

Back when he'd been married to Sherleen, his caring and his efforts to lay everything at his lady love's feet had gone unappreciated. He figured it would be the same for any man who tried to keep Mercedes happy. What could a man give a woman who already had everything, a woman who could easily take care of herself? Nothing. And he needed to remember that.

Brushing cookie crumbs from his hands, he rose to his feet. "We'd better hit the road. I want to get the horses stabled and settled before dark. And I'm sure you need to register at your hotel."

Rising to her feet, Mercedes stared at him as though she could see his lips moving but couldn't hear his words.

"What did you say? A hotel?"

He picked up the plastic wrap that had covered his sandwich, along with his empty soda can. "That's right. We will be staying in the city for the next two nights. You were aware of that, weren't you?"

Frowning, she quickly began to gather up containers of food and shove them inside the picnic basket. "Of course. But I have no intentions of staying in a hotel, motel, bed-and-breakfast or any other place of lodging." She pointed directly at the horse trailer. "We're hauling our living quarters with us. There's no need for me to spend an exorbitant amount of money on a room that would only be used for sleeping."

His jaw dropped. "But I'll be bunking in the trailer."

She shrugged as if his presence was no concern at all to her. And maybe it wasn't, he thought grimly. Maybe those kisses she'd given him at the line shack had been just a game to her.

"So?" she asked. "If I recall correctly, there are three beds. One double and two bunk beds. That's more than enough sleeping area for the both of us."

Sleeping was hardly what Gabe was worried about. If she stayed in the trailer's living quarters with him, he wouldn't just be fighting for sleep, he'd be in a hell of a war to keep his hands off her.

"I seriously doubt Geraldine expects you to be housed in a horse trailer for the next two nights," he began to argue.

Smiling smugly, she placed the last container of food in the basket, then shut the wooden lid over the top. "Apparently you don't know my mother as well as I thought you did. When roundup is going on in the spring and fall, she sleeps on the ground in a bedroll. As far as she's concerned, the trailer is a luxury. And as her daughter, I don't expect more. Understand?"

No. Gabe didn't understand. All this woman had to do was pull out a credit card and she could pay for as many nights as she wanted in the most luxurious hotel in Oklahoma City. But deep down he knew that wasn't her style.

Desperate now, he walked around the table and peered down at her. "Dammit, Mercedes, you know this is different. Why the hell are you trying to be difficult?"

Her little chin pointed up at him in a challenging way. "How is it different?" she demanded. "We're on a job together. Nothing more. Nothing less. That's the way you want it—isn't it?"

"Yes! But—" He paused, then a look of relief washed over his face. "I don't know what the hell I'm arguing with you for. You can have the trailer and *I'll* rent a hotel room."

Her soft lips suddenly doubled together to form a grim line. "No. You can't do that. You need to be near the horses. Their welfare is your responsibility."

Dammit, she was right. He couldn't go off to another part of town and leave her there alone to contend with the horses by herself. If anything should happen to one of them and he wasn't around to deal with the problem, he'd look like an ass or worse.

"You're getting pleasure out of this, aren't you?" he asked tightly.

Biting down on her bottom lip, she glanced away from him. "Pleasure?" she echoed hoarsely. Twisting her head back to him, she stabbed him with an accusing look. "If you'd actually like to know, I can tell you what would give me pleasure. To hear you say that you're glad I'm making this trip with you. That you look forward to having my company for the next couple of nights instead of spending them alone. But admitting to anything close to that would be too much for you, wouldn't it? You couldn't bear to have me thinking that you might actually like me. No, you're scared that might give me the wrong ideas. God forbid, it might even make me grab you and kiss you. Like this."

Before Gabe realized her intentions, she had curled her arms around his neck and plastered her mouth over his. The shock of her actions very nearly caused him to stagger backward, but he managed to catch himself, and soon her lips were working magic on his senses.

For a few reckless moments, he let himself forget that they were standing out in the open at a public place. He forgot that he wasn't supposed to be touching, tasting, giving in to her delicious charms.

He could hear the hot wind whistling past their bodies, the birds above their heads, the speeding traffic somewhere far behind them. But none of those distractions were enough to break the spell of her kiss. It was the sudden hardening of his body that shocked him back to his senses and gave him the will to finally break the contact between them.

Still facing her, he sucked in several long breaths and tried to collect himself while Mercedes's eyelids slowly lifted. Her blue eyes had a smoky sultriness to them as she gazed up at him. The sight made his gut clench, his teeth snap together. He wanted to wring her neck, yet at the same time, he wanted her back in his arms. The war of contrasts waging inside of him was so violent that it made it impossible for him to form words of any kind.

All he could do was turn on his heel and stalk back to the truck.

As for Mercedes, she tried to tell herself that his walking away didn't matter. But it was very hard to ignore the rejection slicing through her with double-edged blades. Still, she wasn't going to let humiliation or tears take her over. No. She wouldn't give the man that much satisfaction.

Slowly, she ambled to the restroom. She took more than enough time to use the facilities, then strolled back out to the picnic table to pick up the basket of remaining food.

After she'd carefully stowed the perishable items in the refrigerator in the living quarters, she secured the door, then climbed back into the cab of the truck.

Once she'd secured her seat belt and settled back for the ride, Gabe flicked her a sardonic look.

"Are you ready now?"

The cutting tone of his voice brought her temper to a low boil, but she refused to let him see it.

"Yes, thank you," she said with prim sweetness.

"Good," he growled as he thrust the transmission into low gear. "Maybe we'll get there before midnight."

Not bothering to make any sort of retort to his barb, Mercedes waited until he'd gotten back onto the highway and was speeding toward Fort Worth before she spoke again, struggling to keep her voice from trembling with anger and hurt.

Staring straight ahead, she muttered forcefully, "If you think I'm going to apologize for that—for kissing you back there—then forget it! At least I'm not trying to hide my feelings—like you!"

From the corner of her eye, she could see his head whip around, his hard gaze fix itself upon the side of her face. Mercedes could only sit there and wonder why he held such magnified importance to her heart. It was as if her happiness, her very life hinged on his every glance, every word, every touch. *Oh, God, don't let me be hurt all over again,* she silently prayed.

"What is that suppose to mean?" he asked sharply.

Making her face as stoic as possible, she turned her head slightly to look at him. "Think about it, Gabe. You might just figure it out on your own!"

## Chapter Eleven

The remaining miles to Oklahoma City passed for the most part in silence. With Gabe doing little more than glaring at the highway ahead of them, Mercedes used the time to read a paperback book she'd brought with her.

Mercedes was greatly relieved when they reached the sale barn where the auction would be taking place. The stress of being cooped up with a reluctant traveling companion, along with sitting in one spot for hours on end, had utterly drained her.

Across from the massive building, several acres of manicured lawn were equipped with RV and trailer hook-ups. Gabe chose an out-of-the-way spot that was shaded with a huge sycamore tree, and after he'd parked and hooked up the utilities to the living quarters, Mercedes helped him unload the horses and remove their goggles.

Since they were already privy to the stall numbers that their horses had been assigned, they took them directly to the barn, Gabe leading three and Mercedes the other two.

Without him saying anything, she understood that he didn't want her help with any of the actual hands-on care of the horses. But she didn't let that prevent her from hanging around until each animal was groomed, fed, watered and settled down for the night.

"I'm going over to the sales office and check in," Mercedes told him after the last horse was fed. "Would you like to come with me?"

Without looking at her, he bent down and picked up two black feed buckets. "No. That's your department."

Growing more aggravated by the minute, Mercedes closed her eyes and pinched the bridge of her nose. "If I'd stayed home like you wanted me to, it would have been *your* department," she couldn't stop herself from reminding him.

Rising to his full height, he glared at her. "Look, if you don't want to go to the office and let someone know that we've arrived with our horses, then I'll do it."

Her eyes popped open. "That's not what I said! I was inviting you to go with me. I don't know my way around this place any more than you do. I thought it would be nice if we could search for the office together. But I guess that's asking too much of you." She gritted her teeth. Before he could utter a word, she turned on her heel and headed toward the exit of the barn.

Along the way, sellers were tending to their horses, while potential buyers were strolling, catalog in hand, from one stall to the next. When a hand caught her from behind and prevented her forward progress, she expected to turn around and see an old acquaintance, someone who had spotted her and wanted to say hello. Instead, Gabe was standing a step behind her, a faintly sheepish expression on his face.

"What's wrong?" she demanded, knowing he wouldn't have come after her unless there was a problem.

His gaze dropped from hers to the dirt beneath their boots. "Nothing is wrong," he said gruffly. "I changed my mind. We'll go to the office together."

Not feeling the least bit appeased, especially when he sounded as if he were coughing up nails instead of complying with her wishes, she pulled her arm from his grasp. "I wouldn't knock myself out, if I were you."

That brought his head up, and he stared at her for such a long time that Mercedes began to tremble inside, to warm with the need to get close to him.

"Okay, Mercedes, I'm sorry if you think I'm being difficult. This tension between us is not what I want. We have two more long days together ahead of us. We can't spend it fighting and snarling."

"I'm glad you see it that way," she said softly. "There was no reason to let one little kiss make you so angry."

His jaw grew rigid. "I suppose you've forgotten it?"

As she looked into his eyes, she felt her upper body gravitating toward his, but she quickly snapped herself to a ramrod-straight posture.

"No. And I hope you haven't, either."

He sucked in a long breath, then fastened a tight hold on her upper arm. "C'mon. Let's get this over with. I'm hungry and tired and I want this day to be over with."

Mercedes wanted to tell him that he certainly knew how to stroke a girl's ego, but she didn't. For now, he was by her side—she didn't want to say or do anything to change that.

Thirty minutes later, they left the office and stepped back outside. Gabe suddenly realized there was no way he could go to a restaurant without inviting her to join him. Sitting across the dinner table from her wasn't something he relished. After that kiss she'd whammed him with that afternoon, he didn't know what to expect from her. And he'd just as soon eat in peace than to constantly be on guard. But he wasn't a complete heel, no matter how much her company disturbed him.

As they walked away from the sale barn, he said, "There are several restaurants across the highway. Are you ready for dinner?"

Fully expecting her to latch on to his arm and give him a bright smile, she surprised him by shaking her head. "No thank you, Gabe. You go ahead. I'm tired. I'll just grab a bite from the leftovers I put in the fridge."

Instead of the happy relief he should have been feeling, Gabe was deflated. "Oh. Well, I guess I'll see you later—back at the trailer."

Nodding, she turned to leave. "Yes. Have a nice dinner."

Gabe watched her walk off and wondered why he felt as though half of him had been whacked away. Then, muttering a self-deprecating curse under his breath, he headed in the opposite direction.

Five minutes later, he was inside a large steak house, seated in a red-cushioned booth, waiting for a waitress to arrive. When a tall woman with dark auburn hair, carrying a glass of ice water and a menu, approached his table, he glanced at her face, then cast a second, closer glance.

"Caroline, is that you?"

The waitress paused, carefully studying him as she placed the water and menu on the table. "Gabe," she said finally, smiling with fond recognition. "Gabe Trevino! My word, I never expected to see you walk in this place. How are you?"

Caroline Myers had grown up in Grulla. The two of them had attended the same school, and she and her family had lived only two blocks away from Gabe and his uncle. They'd been acquaintances for years, but shortly after he and Sherleen had divorced, he'd heard that Caroline had left town. Until now, he'd not seen her and had thought of her only in passing.

"I'm fine. I'm up here for the horse auction," he told her. "What about you? You live around here?"

She gave a negligent shrug. "Yeah. Guess here is as good as anywhere."

The woman looked much older than her thirty-five years. There were lines around her mouth and eyes that bespoke of fatigue and worries. Like him, Caroline had grown up poor. He'd managed to pull himself up the rungs to a more comfortable life, but it appeared that his old friend was still stuck. That saddened him.

"You must be doin' great," she said as she grabbed a pad from a pocket on her uniform and pulled out the pencil resting above her ear. "I hear some of those horses are worth a small fortune. You know, the kind that rich folks buy. What are you doin'? Buyin' or sellin'?"

"Selling. For a ranch that I work for."

She rested her hip against the edge of the table as she studied him with open curiosity. "Oh. You still down in Texas?"

"Not at Grulla. A little north of there. You still with Gilbert?"

The corners of her mouth turned downward. "No. I finally wised up and divorced him. He wasn't like you, Gabe. He was no good through and through." She let out a long breath, then gave him a halfhearted smile. "I'd better take your order, or you'll never get to eat."

He picked up the menu and, after quickly scanning the dinner options, ordered a rare ribeye steak with fries, tossed salad and coffee. After she'd jotted it all down on a small pad and walked away, he wondered what Mercedes would think of his old friend. That she was coarse and uneducated? That Caroline was far beneath her? No. One thing he'd learned about Mercedes was that she treated everyone the same. From the dirtiest cowhand to her mother's senator beau, they were all simply people who deserved equal respect.

*So why do you think she's playing with you, Gabe? Why do you think her kisses couldn't be the real thing? She doesn't think she's better than you.*

Pestered by the little voice prodding him with questions he didn't want to consider, he purposely turned his mind back to Caroline. He was glad she'd ditched her husband. It had been no secret in Grulla that the man abused her and, frankly, Gabe had never understood why she'd stayed with him. But he knew that love made people toss away their pride and common sense. He was a prime example. For three years, he'd acted like a trained seal, jumping through hoops just to make Sherleen happy, and all the while she'd controlled their finances and made important decisions behind his back. She'd excluded him from all the things a husband and wife should have decided together. Because she hadn't needed him. Nor loved him. Hell, she'd not known what love meant.

He was trying to wipe that dark thought from his mind when he looked up to see Caroline returning with his coffee. After she'd placed it on the table, she gestured to the empty seat across from him. "Mind if I sit down a minute? There's no one else eating in my area right now."

He motioned for her to take a seat. "I'd be glad for your company," he said.

With a wan smile, she brushed off the front of her black uniform, then settled herself in the cushioned seat.

As she folded her work-roughened hands upon the table-top, Gabe said, "It's been a long time since we were in high school. I always thought you'd wind up working as a graphic artist for some big company. I remember you were always good at art."

She laughed as though his suggestion was as absurd as reaching up and plucking a star from the sky. "Oh, Gabe, there wasn't any way that I could have ever gone to college. That kind of life wasn't meant for me."

Caroline's mother had sold tacos and tamales for extra money for the family. Her father had worked as a mechanic for a car dealership in town. They'd been good, hardworking people, but paying for their daughter to attend college had never been in their plans.

"You're still young," he suggested. "It's not too late."

She smiled wanly, then quickly changed subject. "I was sorry to hear about you and Sherleen. But I honestly never did think she suited you, Gabe. Too snooty, in my opinion."

Gabe chuckled. "I wished you'd been around to tell me that sooner." He looked at her. "So are you married now, Caroline?"

She shook her head in a resigned way. "No," she said with a wistful sigh, then her eyes suddenly lit up with joy. "But I have a son now. And you know, he makes everything worthwhile. You got any kids, Gabe?"

He reached for his coffee and wondered why her question left an empty feeling inside him. "No," he answered. "I'm on my own."

Thirty minutes later, Mercedes was sitting at the tiny table inside the trailer when Gabe opened the door and stepped inside. As he looked her way, she unconsciously wrapped her fingers tightly around the mug of coffee she'd been drinking.

"Find something good to eat?" she asked.

He nodded. "Steak. What about you?"

"I dug into the cold fried chicken." She watched as he took off his hat and placed it on the top bunk bed. "I'm sorry you had to eat alone. I guess the trip tired me more than I thought."

He moved over to join her at the table and she suddenly realized how tiny the trailer space seemed now that he was inside it. His presence was so huge she felt as if she were squashed against the walls and struggling for breath. Had she been crazy to insist on sleeping here with him? She'd wanted him to see that she wasn't a pampered princess, but maybe she could have proven it another way. Like this, she probably wouldn't be able to shut her eyes all night.

"Don't worry about it," he said. "I ended up having company anyway."

She darted a glance at his face. It wasn't often that she saw him without his cowboy hat and her gaze glided with appreciation over the thick black waves dipping over his forehead.

"Oh? You ran into a rancher or horseman that you're acquainted with?"

"No." He eased down on the small bench seat facing hers. "Actually, it was a woman. An old friend from Grulla. We grew up on the same street, a couple of blocks from each other."

Her brows arched with curiosity. "What a small world."

"Yeah. She's a waitress in the steak house where I had dinner. She says she lives somewhere around here now."

"Does she have a family?"

"A son. But she told me she was divorced now. I was relieved to hear it. Her ex used to abuse her."

"You don't look all that relieved," Mercedes commented. In fact, she couldn't remember ever seeing such a defeated expression on his face before and it troubled her greatly. No matter how cutting or indifferent his behavior, she still wanted

Gabe to be happy. Was that the way it felt when you really loved someone? she wondered.

He sighed. "I guess seeing Caroline reminded me of times I'd sooner forget. She's been poor all her life, Mercedes. And the hell of it is, she always will be, unless she plucks up enough courage to make a change in her life."

Reaching across the tiny table, she covered his hand with hers. "If she needs help, Gabe, I'm sure we can find a spot for her at the ranch. If you'd like, I could go talk with her."

Surprise flickered in his eyes. "You'd do that?"

"Of course. We could help her with housing and child care, too. That might be enough to allow her to work on her education, or whatever she might need."

His gaze dropped to her hand and her heart began to thud with awareness. The two of them were so alone, cocooned together for the night. How could she not touch him? Show him how very much she wanted him?

"That's very kind of you, Mercedes."

"I'd like to think someone would reach out to me if I was in her position," she said quietly.

His gray eyes met hers. "Why do you have to be so nice? Why can't you go around with your nose stuck in the air and your mind on yourself?"

She laughed softly. "Would you really like for me to be that way?"

He grimaced. "It would make it a hell of a lot easier for me not to like you."

The corners of her pink lips turned upward. "Does that mean you *do* like me? A little?"

A wry expression twisted his features. "I have my weak moments, Mercedes. You know that."

Moments. Yes, there had been moments when he'd held her

in his arms, kissed her as though there were nothing in the world he wanted more. But those times were too few and far between for Mercedes's liking.

"I'm not sure I like being called a weakness," she said.

Sighing roughly, he started to pull his hand from beneath hers. As his arm moved, so did the cuff of his shirt, and Mercedes's gaze zeroed in on the thick welt of scars wrapping around his wrist and running beneath the fabric of his shirtsleeve.

At the last moment, before he could pull completely away from her, she caught his fingers and held on tightly. "Where did you get these, Gabe?"

He outwardly winced as she ran the tip of her forefinger over one of the thick scars.

"It doesn't matter where I got them," he said flatly.

Not to be deterred, she asked, "Do you have more of them?"

He shot her with a pointed glare. "Do you really think that's any of your business?"

Her chin thrust forward. "Yes. I want to know."

Without warning, he abruptly rose to his feet and began to unbutton his shirt with short, angry jerks.

Stunned, Mercedes stared in silence as he pulled the fabric apart, then slipped it over his broad shoulders. The dim, overhead light gleamed across his bronze skin and lathed the mounds and valleys of his hard muscles with gray shadows.

Slowly, slowly, her gaze traveled from his neck down his chest to the flat male nipples decorating the heavy muscles, to the patch of dark hair growing between, the corded abs and the lean waist circled by the waistband of his jeans.

Perfect. Utterly perfect, she thought. And then her breath caught in her throat as she moved her attention to his arms. The biceps were the image of pure strength, his forearms long, sinewy cords—striped with a web of jagged scars.

"If that's not enough to sicken you, there's more," he said curtly, then turned his back toward her.

As she noted the same similar scars on his shoulders, she swallowed at the thickness building in her throat. "Oh." She breathed the one word of dismay. "Oh, Gabe. How did that happen?"

Turning back, he eased down on the seat. "I don't talk to anyone about this, Mercedes. Why do you think I should tell you?"

She swallowed again. "Because I care. Because you matter to me."

"Yeah," he said dryly. "I've heard that before."

Mercedes didn't say anything more. After all, if he couldn't accept her simple words for what they were, arguing with him would be pointless.

Long moments passed as she waited. Then, with a heavy groan, he thrust his arms out toward her as though he dared her to take a closer look.

Not about to shy away, Mercedes leaned forward and placed her fingers gently upon one marked wrist.

"Mercedes," he said thickly, "those scars don't just remind me of an accident, of pain and months of healing. When I look at them, I see a fire. The fire that took my parents' lives."

Horrified, she stared at him. "And you were in the fire, too?"

Resigned to telling her the whole story, he nodded. "I was ten, almost eleven years old at the time. By then, my sisters were married and gone. It was only me and my older brother, Joseph, living at home with our parents, but the night of the fire, Joe was staying over at a friend's house.

"I woke up coughing and it took me a minute to realize the room was full of smoke. I jumped out of bed and jerked open the door to run to my parents' room, but the flames were already eating through the walls and the ceiling."

The image sent chills down Mercedes's spine. "How far were you from your parents' room?"

His jaw rigid, he shook his head. "The house was very small, Mercedes. I couldn't have been more than ten steps from their bedroom door. But a wall of flames stood between me and them."

Her fingers tightened on his wrist. "What did you do? How did you get out?"

"I retraced my steps to the opposite side of the house where the flames hadn't yet reached and went out a window. I was hoping by some miracle that my parents had made it out and I'd find them standing in the yard. But on the other hand, I knew that neither of them would have left the house without me." He paused long enough to wipe a hand across his face. "When I didn't find them there, I began to yell to wake the neighbors, then grabbed a ladder and climbed through a window to my parents' bedroom."

Mercedes gasped. "You could have been killed!"

His gray eyes were stark as they settled on her face. "Could you stand by and watch your parents die without trying to do something to save them?"

The desperation of what he must have been feeling struck her hard, and all she could do was shake her head.

He went on. "Neither could I. So I had to try. But the room was black with smoke and the heat of the flames felt like my whole body was being seared. I couldn't see any sign of my dad, but I finally managed to spot my mother. She was lying near the door that led to the hallway. I was trying to reach her to drag her out when part of the ceiling fell between us. Much of it landed on my back and crashed me to the floor. That's the last thing I remember until I woke up a few minutes later on the lawn."

"How did you get out?" Mercedes asked in amazement. "The smoke inhalation would have been more than enough to kill you, much less the burning debris."

"Apparently our next-door neighbor had heard the commotion and came out just in time to see me crawl through the window. If he hadn't come after me, I would have perished with my parents."

Gabe had gone through a living nightmare, Mercedes thought sickly. He'd only been a child, yet he'd risked his own life to save his parents. It was no wonder he hid his scars from the world. He probably wanted to hide them from himself, too, so he wouldn't have to relive the loss of his parents over and over.

After a stretch of silence, she asked, "Did the authorities ever figure out what started the fire?"

He nodded. "Wiring in the attic. It was old and needed to be replaced. Something, probably a mouse, caused it to short out and shower sparks over the rafters. The whole thing originated over my parents' bedroom."

Tears suddenly burned her throat. "I don't have to ask about your folks to know that they were good people. I'm so sorry you lost them, Gabe."

He glanced away from her. "My father's name was Franco. He worked all his life as a carpenter, building fine houses for the well-to-do, but never earned enough to build one for himself and his family."

"Tell me about your mother," she urged softly.

He rose from the seat and moved the few steps to the door. A tiny window was framed in the upper part of the aluminum panel and though he was gazing beyond the glass pane, she knew that he wasn't really seeing the things outside the trailer.

From where she sat, his eyelids appeared to be closed and she could see the muscles work in his throat as he swallowed with obvious difficulty.

The fact that he still felt such loss for his loved ones didn't surprise her. She'd sensed, from the very first moment he'd whirled her around the dance floor, that he was a man of complex layers and deep passions. She was seeing that part of him now, and the hurt he was feeling was arcing into her, filling her with an ache to ease his heart.

"Her name was Jenna," he said huskily. "She was Irish with chestnut hair and gray eyes. Dad always called her his cactus rose. She had a sweet singing voice, but that never earned her a paycheck, just a spot on the church choir. She took in ironing and sewing to help support the family. And most all of that went to us kids for our needs. When our house burned, she probably had five changes of clothes hanging in the closet. But she never complained, Mercedes."

He turned his head to look at her, and Mercedes was struck by the bleakness on his face.

"I caught her crying in the kitchen one time. I guess she thought no one was around to see her. She was standing in front of the refrigerator, staring at the empty shelves. Can you imagine crying over an empty refrigerator?"

She felt sick for him. "I'd be lying if I said yes. I've never had to worry about my next meal. Or how I was going to feed my children."

He let out a heavy breath of air. "I vowed then that I was going to grow up and change things for her. I was going to make enough money to make her life easy. I didn't get that chance." Regret shadowed his eyes and twisted his lips. "Hell, I couldn't make anything better for her. I couldn't even drag her from that burning bedroom. She lived and died with nothing."

Rising from her seat, Mercedes picked up his shirt. She moved over to where he stood and draped the garment over his bare shoulders.

"You're wrong, Gabe," she whispered gently. "She had the things that matter the most. She had a family that loved her. She had you."

## *Chapter Twelve*

When Gabe woke the next morning, Mercedes was not in the trailer.

He glanced at the wristwatch he'd not bothered to remove last night and let out a groan. He'd not expected to sleep at all last night, much less sleep later than usual.

Slipping a hand through his tousled hair, he glanced at the bed where Mercedes had slept. She'd been so close that if he'd stretched his arm in her direction, he could have touched her. But he hadn't. Instead, he'd lain there, listening to her breathing and thinking about her reaction to his parents' tragedy.

Sharing that part of his life with her had ripped him open, past the scars on his skin, down to the raw wounds that had never healed. Showing her that vulnerable part of him had changed him, drawn him to her in a way he'd never expected.

Suddenly the physical attraction he felt for her had been overridden by something deeper, something stronger than the sexual urge to touch her, make love to her. He'd felt incredibly close to her, happy that he had her company, and solaced by the fact that she understood the loss of his parents.

*Watch it, Gabe, or your heart is going to start leading you around instead of your head. And that's when you're going to get it broken in so many pieces you'll never get it put back together.*

Trying to push that unsettling thought from his mind, Gabe rose from the bed and reached for his boots. He didn't have time to think about anything except getting the horses ready for the sale ring.

Five minutes later, he was washed, dressed and stepping outside when he glanced around to see Mercedes, a white paper sack in her hand, walking toward him.

"Good morning," she said cheerfully when she got within hearing distance. "I'm glad I got back before you headed to the barn. I've got hot coffee and breakfast."

Even before she opened the sack, he could smell the delicious aroma of hot biscuits and coffee. His stomach growled, insisting he had to take five minutes to fill it before he went to work.

He inclined his head toward the sack. "Where did you get that?"

"Over at the steak house. Let's get a pair of lawn chairs and eat out here," she suggested. "The morning is beautiful."

Yes, the sky was clear and blue, the air dry and pleasant. A warm smile was on her face, and Gabe's heart did an odd little dance every time he looked at her. Dammit.

He grabbed chairs from the bed of the truck and quickly set them up beneath the sycamore tree. Once they were both seated, Mercedes began to pull out the food.

As she handed him a biscuit and sausage sandwich, she said, "While I was at the restaurant, I talked to your friend, Caroline."

He bit into the bread and meat. "If she's working this early, she must have very long shifts."

"She was filling in for someone who had called in sick," Mercedes explained.

He took the foam cup she offered him and pulled off the plastic lid. "I didn't tell you her name. How did you figure out who she was?"

"Intuition, I suppose. I asked her if she knew you and that was all it took." Her blue eyes studied him thoughtfully as she chewed her food. "Before I left the restaurant, I gave her the Sandbur's number and instructions to speak to Cook."

Even though she'd mentioned helping Caroline, the fact that she'd already put things into motion surprised him. "For a job?"

"What else?" she asked with an indulgent smile. "You implied that she needed help."

"Yes," he reasoned. "But that isn't your problem."

"I don't see it as a problem. The ranch can always use good help. And if she's your friend, that's enough reference for me."

Gabe didn't know what to think or say. Had she done this to actually help Caroline or just to impress him?

*Hell, Gabe, for once in your life can you quit viewing everything with a cynical eye? No matter what Mercedes's motives, she's done a good thing. Accept it for that.*

"Thank you, Mercedes."

She smiled. "My pleasure."

Once their simple breakfast was over, Gabe left to care for the horses while Mercedes spent the remainder of the day schmoozing with rich buyers and taking note of how the auction was run. Her mother had understated the grandeur of the event, and she'd been greatly surprised when she'd entered the sale barn to see huge baskets of cut roses and other fresh flowers lining the area where the horses would be shown.

The men working the auction were all dressed in dark suits and ties and the registry catalogs handed out to potential buyers were more like glossy magazines rather than facts printed on rough paper.

As for herself, she was glad she'd thought to bring a Western-cut pantsuit that she sometimes wore on dressy occasions. She'd also taken pains with her makeup and hair. She wanted to look her best when she represented the Sandbur.

Yet as she milled among the privileged crowd and introduced herself to both buyers and sellers, she realized she'd much rather be in the horse barn with Gabe, wearing her old jeans and boots and getting her hands dirty. But even if she told him that, Mercedes doubted he would believe her. He wanted to set her apart in everything, as though they could never be on the same level.

Mercedes remained near the sale ring until the hammer fell on the last lot number auctioned for the day, then left the building. When she reached the camping area where their rig was parked, she found Gabe outside, charcoaling wieners on a small pit.

"Mmm. Those smell good," she declared as she walked up behind him. "Been here long?"

He glanced over his shoulder at her, then turned his attention back to the sizzling planks of meat. "Only a few minutes."

With a tired sigh, she pulled up a lawn chair and sank into it. As she stretched her long legs out in front of her, she said, "The auction producers are having a shindig tonight. Cocktails and dancing at a ritzy downtown hotel. We're invited."

He let out a mocking snort. "You're invited. Not me."

Mercedes pushed her fingers through the hair at her temples. "Wrong. The both of us were invited."

"Sorry. I'm not up to that sort of—job."

"Thanks for making attending an event with me sound like a job," she said dryly.

"Don't miss it on my account. I'm sure you'd enjoy the evening. You'll feel right at home with those people."

"So would you. *You've* worked with enough of them."

He began to fork the franks onto a paper plate. "Wrong again, Mercedes. I worked *for* them."

The moment she'd walked up, she'd been struck by the fact that he was wearing a plain white T-shirt. His usual long-sleeved shirt was gone and the scars on his forearms were exposed. Apparently he was finally beginning to feel comfortable around her. At least, comfortable enough not to hide the marks of tragedy on his forearms. The idea made everything inside her smile.

"Don't bother splitting hairs," she commented. "And I'm not about to go. Unless you go with me—as my date."

He ran a hand across the back of his neck, then rolled his head to relieve the tension in his shoulders. "All right. If you really want to go, I suppose I can put on my best and pretend, for your sake. But I'm going to be honest and tell you that I'm beat. I'd rather stay here and relax."

It was almost shocking to Mercedes the pleasure his response evoked in her. He'd be willing to go. For her sake. But more importantly, he'd been honest with his own wishes, instead of putting up a pretense just to please her. And that was much more than John or Drew had ever given her.

Rising to her feet, she joined him at the small brick pit and peered over his shoulder at the last two franks grilling over the charcoal. "I'm glad you said that, because I don't want to go, either. So are you going to invite me to share your supper?"

"I'll share."

She pecked a swift kiss on his cheek, then turned and rushed toward the trailer. "I'm going to change. I'll be right back!"

Thirty minutes later, he watched her swallow the last bite of her second hot dog, then lick the remaining mustard from the tips of her fingers.

The simple yet sensual act only added to his awareness of the woman. He found his gaze wandering for the ump-teenth time over the smooth, tanned skin exposed by her jean shorts and skimpy tank top. This evening was one of the few times he'd seen her out of her cowboy boots, and he found that even her dainty toes with their bright pink nails mes-merized him.

"I'm beginning to think you could compete with Cook," she told him. "That was great."

"There are still a couple of franks left if you want another."

With a contented groan, she slid her hand across her mid-section. "No thanks. I'm so full I can hardly breathe."

Night was falling fast and he knew he should get up and gather the remains of their supper. But he was loath to move when he was finding such pleasure in watching the long shadows of the evening paint themselves across her shapely body.

A few times today, he'd seen her from a distance, smiling and charming her way through the horsing crowd, most of whom were men. He'd be lying if he tried to deny that he'd been jealous of the interplay between her and the good-looking males of the bunch. Yet at the same time, he had to tell himself that he had no right to feel such an emotion toward the woman. She didn't belong to him. And those precious smiles weren't always directed solely at him.

He pushed away a heavy sigh and asked, "What did you think about the price we got for our two horses today?"

"I was very pleased. The stallion went in the high five

figures and the filly was close to that. I'm sure the whole family will be happy. Especially if the three tomorrow go that well." She slanted him a sidelong glance. "By the way, you did a heck of a job showing both horses. You made them look very good."

Her compliment sent a warm glow through him, one that he desperately tried to ignore. Shaking his head, he said, "I didn't make them look good. They did it all themselves."

She leaned forward and as she did he caught the sweet scent of her perfume drifting on the night wind.

"Do you ever take credit for your work?" she asked.

"When I think I've done something to deserve it."

A grin tugged at her lips. "You know, it's pretty standard for most cowboys to be a little arrogant."

He grunted with amusement. "I'm not a cowboy. I'm a horseman."

He was the epitome of both, Mercedes thought. Yet in many ways, he was no different from the airmen she'd worked with for eight long years. His uniform might be jeans and boots instead of dress blues, but he still had that same toughness, dedication and pride.

"Yes. You are that," she said with sober conviction. Rising to her feet, she stretched her arms above her head. "I think I'll go in and make a pot of coffee. Would you care for some?"

He also stood and began to gather up the remains of their meal. "I'll be there in a few minutes."

His few minutes turned out to be several. Tired of waiting, Mercedes finally poured herself a cup and sat at the small table inside the trailer, sipping the hot drink until Gabe finally entered the tiny space.

"I thought you'd gotten lost on your way to the trash barrel," she teased.

"I went to the barn for one last check on the horses before we retire for the night."

She scooted out of the seat to scrounge around in the cabinet for another mug. "You should have told me your intentions. I could have helped you."

"There wasn't anything to do, except fill their hay mangers."

He was standing directly behind her, so close that if she leaned the slightest bit backward, her shoulders would be touching his chest. Just thinking about having his hard, warm body against hers drugged her senses until she felt as though every movement she was making was in slow motion.

Nervously running the tip of her tongue over her lips, she turned and presented him with the coffee cup. His gray eyes connected with hers and the air around them suddenly seemed to be throwing off erotic sparks.

"Here you go," she said lowly.

"Thanks."

He poured himself some coffee and eased onto one of the benches at the table. Mercedes sat down on the opposite bench and tried to breathe normally as she looked at everything within the eight-foot space except him.

"Have you heard from Geraldine today?" he asked.

She darted a glance at his face. At some point since he'd stepped through the door, he'd removed his hat. Now a hank of black, shiny hair brushed against his eyebrow as his head bent forward over the coffee cup. She desperately wanted to touch it, to spear her fingers into the curls around his ears. Even worse, she wanted to put her mouth over his, to let the dark, erotic taste of him sweep her away.

"No. I don't expect she'll be calling anytime soon. In fact, I hope she totally forgets about us and the ranch. I want this time she has with Wolfe to be special."

The only sound inside the trailer was the faint ticking of an alarm clock, but it was still hard for Mercedes to hear over the blood drumming loudly in her ears. It was impossible to figure why tonight felt so different from the previous one— she only knew that it did. Somehow, she instinctively felt that tonight wasn't for revelations. It was for loving.

He said, "I just hope the guy appreciates Geraldine. She deserves an honorable man."

She peeped at him through her long lashes. "That's very sweet of you to say, Gabe." Then before she could let herself think twice, she reached across the tiny table and gently laced her fingers around his wrist. "And speaking of mothers, I'm— well, I wanted to thank you for sharing your parents' story with me last night. That time in your life can't be easy to talk about."

As she spoke, her fingers moved gently against the uneven surface of the scars on his wrist and his gaze dropped to where she was touching him.

"It's like stepping back into a nightmare," he agreed in a low voice.

His skin was warm and just rough enough to feel very masculine beneath the pads of her fingers. Flattening her hand against his arm, she slid it upward toward his elbow, watching his eyes narrow in response. The subtle reaction pushed her pulse to an even faster rate.

"I like you without long sleeves," she said softly. "I like that you're not trying to hide anything from me."

The corners of his chiseled mouth turned slightly downward. "You like seeing all my flaws?"

"We all have flaws. Inside and out," she whispered. "That's what makes us human."

Something sparked in his eyes and then his hand was suddenly gripping her shoulder, tugging her toward him.

"You don't want to see inside of me," he mouthed against her lips. "It's empty. Very empty."

Like icy drops of rain, anticipation rolled slowly down her spine and shivered in the very depths of her.

"Let me be the judge of that," she murmured. Then, before he decided to back away, she closed the last breath of space between their lips.

The contact was like sticking a match to a bed of dry grass. There was nothing slow, sweet or gentle about the kiss or the violent longing it erupted in Mercedes. With one hand at the back of her head and the other cupping her jaw, he held her fast, forcing her lower body to leave the bench and her upper body to rest upon the tabletop as his lips feasted on hers, his tongue invading the moist confines of her mouth.

In a matter of moments, she was totally lost to him, her mind focused on one thing—getting closer. Having his hands upon her body, his hard strength against her.

Moaning deep in her throat, she thrust her fingers in his hair and tried to match the rough, hungry search of his lips. Somewhere along the way, she felt his hands at the back of her arms urging her up from the bench, and then they were both standing. The front of her body was crushed against his.

She was wrapping her arms around his waist, exploring the warmth of his back through the thin T-shirt when he finally tore his mouth from hers and stared at her in anguish.

"This is all wrong," he muttered. "I can't have you."

Her hand glided over his lean cheek. "Isn't that for me to decide?"

His features twisted as though he were in physical pain and her question was making it a thousand times worse. "We've got to think about tomorrow and the days after that."

A provocative smile curled the corners of her lips as she

brought her forehead against his. "Our days are going to get better, Gabe. Even better than tonight," she promised.

His groan was full of skepticism, but he didn't pull away from her when she pressed her lips back to his. And then nothing either of them had said seemed to matter. With everything inside of her, she wanted this man. If she stopped to worry about tomorrow, then she would miss the love he could be giving her tonight.

To press her point home, she slipped her hands under his shirt and splayed them against his muscled chest. He ripped his mouth from hers and began to press a tiny row of kisses down the side of her neck.

"You don't know what you're doing," he mouthed against her skin. "But I'm tired of fighting you—especially tonight."

His words thrilled her and her heart began to hammer out of control as he caught the hem of her top and began to peel it upward and over her head.

"Oh, Gabe, I do know what I'm doing," she fervently whispered. "All I want is this. You."

The image of making love to her had been going over and over in his mind for weeks, and it was hard to believe that it was actually happening. That he was *letting* it happen. But he had no choice. Not when he was on fire for her and she was melting against him.

Quickly, before sanity could creep into his thoughts, he slipped away her shorts, then dealt even more rapidly with her sexy undergarments. By the time she was standing naked before him, he was on fire, aching to be inside her, to relieve the desire that was wrapping around him, binding him to the charms of her body.

Between kisses on her face and neck and breasts, he somehow managed to shuffle out of his own clothing and kick away his boots. When the cumbersome garments were finally out of the way, he reached for her. "Come here, my lovely," he whispered.

With her hand in his, he stepped backward, drawing her with him until he bumped into the set of bunk beds. He sank onto the bottom mattress and drew her down with him.

The bed was short and narrow, but neither of them noticed. All that Mercedes's senses could register was that she was in his arms. His skin was on fire, bathing her in heat. His lips were on hers, pushing her to a height that she'd not known was possible.

Her hands eagerly raced over his body, familiarizing themselves with every muscle of his back, the scarred tendons in his arms, the bumps of his ribs and the long ridge of his backbone. He was all man and strength, and she wanted to absorb it all, to connect herself to him in every way.

When his hand slipped between the juncture of her thighs, he pulled his head back far enough to peer into her face.

"Are you on any sort of birth control?"

Even though she was a grown woman who'd had a lover before, the question filled her face with heat.

"I— No. This isn't something I—do on a regular basis." Until now, she'd not met any man whom she'd wanted to expose herself to in such an intimate way since John's betrayal, but she didn't want to lay that much importance on the moment and scare him away.

Her short breaths seemed to go on forever as he studied her face. Mercedes's heart slowed with dread as she saw a hint of doubt flicker in his eyes. But just as quickly, it was gone and he gently brushed his knuckles against her cheekbone, making her lips tingle, her eyes close.

"I'll take care of it," he whispered.

He left the bunk and went to find his wallet. Moments later, he returned, his manhood safely sheathed in a condom.

The man wasn't taking any chances, she thought with a tiny pang of regret. But on the other hand, that was good. God knew how much she wanted him. Wanted him for keeps. But not through entrapment. She needed his love, and needed it to be given to her willingly, freely.

Once he rejoined her on the bunk, their bodies became a tangled mass of heated flesh. Mercedes had never had anyone kiss her this hungrily, touch her so boldly or turn her senses to mush. She was nothing without the man, and everything with him. The stroke of his hands empowered her, the feel of his lips upon her sent the very center of her being searching and soaring.

When he finally rolled her onto her back and entered her, Mercedes was stunned with the ferocity of the emotions that stung her from all directions. The physical presence of him inside of her was an incredible sensation, yet it wasn't the reason that her eyes misted with tears, or that her heart felt as though it would burst. She loved this man. Loved him with every fiber of her being.

After his divorce, he'd sworn to always be in control, to never allow anyone or anything to make him give up his will-power and bend him in a direction he didn't want to go. But Mercedes was swiftly dissolving that idea. The feel of her small hands gliding over him, the desperate writhing of her body beneath his, the scent of her and the taste of her smooth skin was turning him into a helpless piece of flesh that he couldn't restrain or direct.

He was hardly a novice at making love to a woman and always before he had found it easy to take his time and push all the right buttons, to give satisfaction before he took it. But with Mercedes there wasn't any plan or artifice. No thinking or maneuvering. His hands, his mind and heart were simply reacting to her. Loving her.

And like a blind man racing toward a promised light, his strokes became quicker, deeper, hungrier. Beneath him, her hips were racing to match his rhythm, her open mouth was hot against his chest, her tongue licking, tasting, driving his senses to places he'd not gone before.

When the end came, he was certain that he was floating above her, that the stars behind his eyes were the same as those twinkling down on the red Oklahoma dirt. Above the deafening roar in his ears, he could hear her ecstatic cries, feel her body clenching around his, and he felt a surge of triumph that she was soaring with him. Like two doves winging upward, together, into the blue, blue sky.

Awareness returned slowly as he sucked long, raspy breaths into his burning lungs. Gradually, the fierce pounding of his heart settled to a rapid thud. His cheek was pressed against her silky blond hair and her damp body was smothered beneath his. The heavenly scent of her swirled about him and her soft breath brushed warmly against his shoulder.

He didn't want to move, to break the connection of their bodies. But he knew he had to relieve her of his weight, so he rolled to his side and took her with him.

She didn't say a word. Instead, her sigh said it for her as she snuggled her cheek against his chest and wrapped an arm around his waist.

Gabe slipped a hand beneath the heavy cape of her hair and stroked the back of her neck, while his mind raced to process what had just taken place between them. His earth had suddenly split open and he was shocked at the free fall he'd taken.

He'd just learned what it was like to make *love* to a woman. And one way or another, he instinctively knew his life would never be the same again.

## Chapter Thirteen

It was late the next evening when the two of them arrived back at the Sandbur. Mercedes was tired, but pleasantly so. The trip coming home had seemed much shorter than going. Maybe because the last three horses had each brought an exceptional price in the sale ring and ended their trip on an even brighter note. Or maybe because making love to Gabe had changed the way the world looked to her. Everything seemed more beautiful, and she'd chattered throughout the whole trip like a songbird on a spring morning.

After Gabe parked the big rig in its regular spot inside a storage shed near one of the cattle barns, Mercedes began to gather up her handbag and the other odds and ends that she'd collected during the trip.

Rolling back into the ranch yard had been sobering to Gabe. Throughout the day, he'd allowed himself to pretend. He'd let himself believe that he and Mercedes could actually be lovers, that somehow their lives could merge without a problem. But returning to Sandbur soil had woken him from that impossible dream. She *owned* part of this ranch. He only *worked* here. And if that wasn't problem enough, who was to say that she would actually be here for much longer? Lex had already hinted to him that he expected her to fly soon. Why should Gabe think any differently? Mercedes hadn't bothered to tell him anything about her future plans or even how she actually felt toward him.

"Wow, I didn't realize I'd picked up so many souvenirs," she commented with a chuckle as she stuffed the last plastic bag into her purse. "I hope my family loves me for all the money I spent on them."

Before he could talk himself out of what he was about to do, he reached over the gearshift and wrapped his fingers around her forearm. The touch brought her head around and the tender smile she gave him pierced him right in the heart.

"Mercedes, I—" All of a sudden his words jammed somewhere inside him and refused to come out.

"You wanted to tell me something?" she prompted gently.

He drew in a long breath and wondered why there was such an aching pressure in his chest. This woman didn't love him. She'd never even hinted that she did. "Uh, yeah. I think before you go to the house that we should talk."

Her smile turned impish and even more provocative. He tried to ignore the charming dimples in her cheeks even though all he wanted to do was lean forward and kiss the pretty grooves bracketing her lips.

"Oh," she said. "Well, if you're wondering about giving Mother a report about the auction, I'll call her tonight. She's going to be very happy with the way things went."

Feeling much sicker than he'd expected to, he shook his

head. All through the trip home, he'd not allowed himself to think about the future. He'd purposely blacked it out so that he could simply enjoy the moment of being with Mercedes. But now reality had hit him and he'd not been prepared for this much pain. How could it hurt to end something that had never really started? Why should breaking away from this woman be any different from those in the past?

*Because you only had sex with them, Gabe. You never made love until last night. Mercedes filled a hole in you. And you don't want to think of feeling that emptiness again, of losing everything she gave you.*

"It's not about Geraldine or the auction." He forced the words from his lips. "I want to talk about you—us."

Her blue eyes widened, then turned dreamy as she leaned slightly toward him. "I hope you're about to invite me out to the line shack tonight," she whispered.

Oh, yes, he could easily imagine her there in his bed, the sheets wet from their sweat, her soft hand resting upon his heart. But he couldn't let that happen. It would only make things harder when she did finally go. And she would go. A woman with her credentials and looks wouldn't stay buried on a dusty Texas ranch forever.

"No. In fact, I—" He looked away from her and swallowed, hating himself for being so weak, for hoping, even in the tiniest way, that she might actually care for him. "Mercedes, last night—what happened between us was a one-time thing. If you were thinking we were going to fall into some sort of relationship, I'm sorry. It can't happen."

She reared back as though he'd struck her. "What do you mean, can't happen?"

He grimaced as pain seeped into places inside him that he'd long believed to be dead. "Just what I said. Us being together can only cause problems. Problems that I don't think either of us want to deal with."

Anger replaced the dismay on her face and her nostrils flared as her gaze raked over him. "You certainly didn't have any problems being with me last night," she accused.

Hot color crept up his neck and onto his jaws. "That was a—lapse in judgment. I let the place, the moment take over. But now that we're back on the Sandbur, I can see things clearly. We're worlds apart. You know it and I know it. To try to fit together would be foolish."

Jerking her arm from his grasp, she glared at him. "What are you doing? Trying to punish me for being the boss's daughter? I can't help it if part of this ranch belongs to me. That's just a happenstance of birth. It should have no bearing on how we feel about each other."

"You're right. It shouldn't matter, but it does. And I—I don't intend to make a second mistake with a woman."

Mistake? Was that how he viewed last night? If she hadn't already been so numb with shock, his words would have sliced her right down the middle.

"If that's how you feel, then why did you sleep with me?" she demanded, her voice wounded and throbbing. "Why did you lie beside me until the sun came up? Why did you act as though you cared? As though you *wanted* to be with me?"

Somewhere during her blast of questions, she began to tremble all over and her eyes misted with tears. Before he could watch her pride crumble right in front of him, she yanked open the door on the truck and climbed to the ground.

She was walking away, fully intending not to say another word to him when his hand came down on her shoulder. Spinning around, Mercedes stared at him in stunned fascination.

"What's the matter? You haven't jabbed me enough? I

suppose you won't be satisfied until you've cut me to shreds." The shock of his sudden about-face was wearing away, and in its place anger and pain was shooting through her like shards of glass. "Why don't you go ahead and put the icing on the cake? Tell me that last night meant nothing to you."

His fingers bit deeply into her shoulder. "Stop it! You're saying things that aren't anywhere near the truth and—"

"And I never should have been so gullible," she interrupted sarcastically. "I guess you think I'm pretty naive for believing that last night was more than just a one-night stand for you. You must have had a nice little chuckle behind my back."

As she watched his rigid jaw relax, tears spilled from the rim of her eyes. Last night she'd been certain she'd felt love in his touch. How had she been so wrong about a man? *Again.*

His fingers reached up and gently touched her cheek. "Nothing about last night was funny—it meant everything to me. But that doesn't change anything."

"Why?"

Glancing away from her, he swallowed. "I know what it feels like to invest your feelings in someone and then have it all smash into nasty little pieces. That's not for me. Not again."

"If you're talking about your wife, then I don't know how you could compare the two of us. I—"

Swinging his gaze back to her, he cut into her words, "I'll tell you how I could make the comparison. Like you, she was beautiful. Sexy. And rich. Her father was the mayor of Grulla, and he came from old oil money. They lived in a mansion on the outskirts of town, they drove luxury cars and traveled anywhere their hearts desired. I knew the moment that I first met Sherleen that she was trouble. But she was so easy on the eyes and it stroked my ego to have someone like her chasing after me." The sneer on his face was directed solely at himself.

"Can you imagine a poor orphan like me catching the eye of someone like her? It was a fool's dream. And yet I let it happen. I let myself believe that she actually loved me and that we could make a life together."

"What happened?" she whispered hoarsely.

"Hell," he snorted, "do you have to ask? She wanted everything that I didn't. A rich social life, traveling, fun and parties."

"You should have known that when you married her."

"Yeah, I should have and I did. But I thought things would change after we became man and wife. Instead, after three months of marriage I was exhausted. When I tried to slow her down, to make her see that I wanted a regular home life, a family with children, she kept promising that things would be different. That she'd settle down and become a better wife, even give me children. And she tried. But it wasn't her style. She was incapable of changing."

"How can you be so sure she wouldn't have changed? People can and do—when they really want to."

He muttered a curse under his breath. "Because all the time she was pretending to be the good wife, she was lying, keeping things from me, seeing people I didn't approve of, going places where a married woman had no business being."

"So what finally ended it for you?"

"I found her hidden birth control pills. We'd been trying for a baby with no success. And she'd been voicing fears that she might be infertile. Infertile, hell," he sneered. "She was doing everything she could to keep from getting pregnant, and lying to me about it."

Mercedes's head swung back and forth in amazement. No wonder he didn't want a woman in his life. His wife had betrayed him in the worst kind of way.

His ugly revelation had Mercedes viewing him in a whole different light and understanding so much more. Instead of frustration, she felt an aching need to assure him, to make him see that he'd never experience anything like that again. Not with her.

"Why did she want to get married in the first place?" Mercedes asked. "Obviously she wasn't ready to be a wife."

"I thought she was marrying me for love, for all the traditional reasons that couples do. But now when I look back, I think that for Sherleen, our short marriage was all just one more adventure. From the time she was born, her parents made sure she got what she wanted. And for some reason, she wanted me."

Stupid, selfish woman. The three words were on the tip of her tongue, but Mercedes bit them back. To say them would only make him feel worse. Like her—she didn't want or need to be reminded that she'd been foolish enough to pick a loser or a user, either.

"What happened to her after your divorce?"

He grimaced. "She went running back to her family. And with me out of the way, she took up her single life again. Now, I don't know or care where she is."

With a heavy sigh, Mercedes turned away from him and ran a hand through her tousled hair. She supposed that she should be totally insulted that he could compare her to such a woman. But because of the betrayals she suffered with two different men, she understood how deep a hurt like that could run, how it often made common sense impossible to see. Telling him that she wasn't like Sherleen would be useless. He had to see that truth for himself. He had to learn to trust all over again. But how long would it be before that happened? Maybe it would never happen, she thought sickly.

Turning back to him, she said bleakly, "I'm very sorry that happened to you, Gabe. But I'm even sorrier that you think the same thing would happen with me."

Something flickered on his face, but she didn't hang around to read his expression or to wait for any sort of reply. She turned and walked out of the shed before he could see the tears streaming down her face.

More than a week later, long after sundown, Gabe was in the training pen, subtly cuing a horse to side pass, when he spotted Lex climbing onto the top rung of the fence. Figuring the man had come to talk, Gabe nudged the horse over to where Mercedes's brother sat with his hat pushed back and an ever-present grin on his face.

"I see you made it back from Florida," Gabe greeted.

"Yeah, thank God. If I don't see another rod and reel in the next twenty years, I'll be a happy man."

"Too much fishing, huh?"

"Too much everything," he conceded with a chuckle. "But I made a nice sell on a couple of bulls, so I guess the trip was worth it. I heard the horses did very nicely at auction. Way to go, Gabe. Cordero's going to be jealous when he hears how well you've settled into his boots."

Gabe's smile was little more than halfhearted as he crossed his forearms over the saddle horn. "I could never settle into Cordero's boots. We don't wear the same size."

Lex laughed, then studied him a bit closer. "I stopped by to see if anyone had told you about the roundup next week. I figured you'd want time to pick out some ponies to take. Since we'll be doing a lot of roping and branding, it's a good learning experience for them."

Gabe nodded. "Thanks for letting me know. I'll certainly have a string ready. I have several two-year-olds that I'd like to work."

Along with the falling sun, the wind had also died, leaving the evening hot and muggy. Gabe lifted his hat from his head and wiped the sweat from his face with the back of his sleeve. Beneath him, the horse stomped at a pestering nit fly.

He'd already put in fifteen hours today. He should have gone home when the last of the wranglers had left for the bunkhouse, but home only made him think of Mercedes. He still didn't know how to fight her haunting memory. Still didn't know how to rub out the dull pain that breaking away from her had left in his heart.

"I guess I should also warn you," Lex went on, "that all the family goes on roundup, including Mother. In fact, if anyone isn't out of his bedroll by daylight, she'll get him out with a pitcher of water in the face."

Gabe looked at him. "You say all the family goes?"

"Well, I'm not sure about the women. There are so many new babies in the family, it's hard to say. But I think Juliet will be coming along with Matt. And if Ripp can get off duty, he and Lucita will go so that Marti can enjoy the experience of riding and camping out."

*And what about Mercedes?* Gabe wondered. These past days, he'd spotted her coming and going from her little office, but he'd not approached her or attempted to talk to her. Any work he'd needed for her to do, he'd left with written instructions on her desk, long before her workday started.

It was a cowardly way to deal with her, he realized. But there was nothing he could say to make things better, and to try would only make things worse. He realized she saw him as a bastard who had used her. He hated that and hated himself for ever having made love to her in the first place.

As though Lex could read his mind, he suddenly added, "I'm not sure about Mercedes. She's been acting strangely these days. I don't know what's wrong with her, but it's plain she's not happy. I wouldn't be a bit surprised if she takes that job offer from D.C."

Gabe felt as though Lex had thrown ice water over his head. "D.C.?"

Lex nodded. From the man's expression, he didn't seem all that pleased about the news. Gabe had always gotten the impression that Lex was very close to his sister and resented the fact that she'd stayed away for so long in the Air Force.

"Yeah," Lex said. "At the Pentagon. Some sort of intelligence gathering for Homeland Security. She'd be serving her country well, I can admit that. But I'll be honest with you, Gabe. I'm selfish. I want her here. This is where she belongs. Not behind some desk with military men snapping orders at her. Hell, if that's what makes her happy, I can snap plenty at her."

Gabe felt sick to his stomach. How long had Mercedes known about this job offer? While they'd been in Oklahoma? If so, she'd kept it from him. One more thing proving she wasn't a woman who really wanted to share her life with him. "Well, that kind of work has been a part of her life for a long time, Lex. Maybe it's in her blood—like ranching is in ours."

Muttering a curse, Lex began to climb down from his seat. "Females. They never know what they want or how much they can hurt us."

With a backward wave, Lex walked away. As Gabe watched him head toward the big house, he wondered why God had led him to this ranch in the first place. To hurt him all over again?

It didn't make sense. But then, nothing about love ever did.

* * *

The next morning found Mercedes sitting at her desk. A mound of tasks were waiting to get done, but instead of throwing herself into her job, she was on the telephone, listening to her sister call her a coward.

"It doesn't matter how much you badger me, Nicci," Mercedes replied firmly. "I'm not going to go begging the man— for anything. He doesn't want me in his life. Period."

The irritated breath that Nicci let out was loud enough to be heard over the phone. "I didn't think I wanted to be in Ridge's life, either. But he proved me very wrong. That's what you have to do with Gabe. He *needs* to know that you love him. At least tell him so."

"Nicci, I'm not good at expressing my feelings to a man. And one of these days, I'll tell you why. John is only half the reason. For right now, just trust me when I tell you that I've learned that telling a man things—intimate things—can end up making a woman very humiliated."

"Being humiliated is not nearly as bad as being alone. And you know that I'm speaking from experience."

Passing a hand over her forehead, Mercedes glanced out the office window. So far this morning, Gabe had not appeared within her view. But that didn't mean he wasn't close by, and the thought of confronting him again made her tremble all over. For the past week and a half, she'd literally pined for the man. The night they'd spent together in Oklahoma continually drifted through her mind like a haunting refrain she couldn't mute.

She'd fallen in love with him that night. No—that wasn't true. She'd fallen in love with him well before that. She just hadn't known it until their bodies had connected, until she'd slept beside him and he'd given her kisses for breakfast. That time with him had been euphoric and had given her a glimpse into how wonderful their life could be together, if he would only give them a chance.

When they'd arrived back on the ranch and he'd made that abrupt turnaround, she couldn't have been more shocked. He'd given her no hint or sign that he'd had plans to end things between them. If anything, he'd been more kind and gentle on the way home than he'd ever been to her. She'd been blissfully unaware that her happiness had been one-sided.

"Yes, I know that if anyone knows about a broken heart and a worthless man, you do. But at least you have a wonderful man who loves you now. And a beautiful daughter." Groaning, she pressed fingertips to her closed eyelids. "Oh, Nicci, why did I have to fall in love with a man who doesn't want me? Maybe I should leave. Take the job in D.C."

There was a long pause before Nicci finally replied. "That isn't what you want."

"No," Mercedes choked in agreement. "That part of my life is over. I want the man I love. I want us to have a home and children."

"Then get off the phone and do something about it."

Before Mercedes could make any sort of reply, she heard the line click and knew that her sister had said all she was going to say on the matter. And it was enough.

Dropping the phone back in its cradle, Mercedes rose from the leather chair and hurried out of the room. For the past week and a half, Gabe had deliberately ignored her, but she was about to change that.

She didn't find Gabe outside where he worked, so she headed for his office.

By the time she reached the door, her heart was pounding with nervous adrenaline and her hands were sweaty. She wiped them down the sides of her sundress then knocked on the door.

"Come in."

Taking a deep breath, she stepped inside. He was sitting in front of the computer, a telephone crammed against his ear. He was dressed all in dark denim, and beneath the overhead lighting, his black hair gleamed like rich coal. Sensuality seeped from the man like heat from the sun. Yet as she looked at him, she realized there was so much more to him. Beneath all that tough brawn, he was a man who'd loved and lost, fought and scratched his way up. He'd endured rejection and loneliness. Just like her.

As she moved into the room, he glanced up casually, then instantly stiffened the moment he saw that it was her.

"Uh, there's something I need to tend to, Jim. I'll call you back in a few minutes," he said to the person on the phone. "Yeah. Thanks."

After hanging up the receiver, he leaned back in his chair as though he were a principal and she a naughty student waiting to confess her wrongdoing.

"Sorry," she said. "I always seemed to be interrupting."

With slow, deliberate movements, he reached for a pencil. She wanted to tell him he didn't have to worry about taking notes. She planned on making everything crystal clear.

"If you're here about the list for Matt's auction," he said curtly, "I don't have it ready."

Summoning all the courage she could find, Mercedes walked over to his desk and rested a hip on the corner. All the while, she could feel his eyes sliding over her face and neck, down the thrust of her bosom and on to her thigh. Desire snaked through her, reminding her of the deep effect the man had on her.

"I'm not here about the list."

His gray eyes traveled back to her face. In their depths, she saw a gentle warning to back away, to leave him and his emotions alone. She stood her ground and clung to her sister's advice. *He needs to know how much you love him. And you need to find the courage to open up to him, to trust him to be different from the men who hurt you.*

He said, "If this is personal, I—"

"I know," she interrupted. "You don't want to hear it. But I'm going to say it anyway. I've had a job offer. It's a prestigious position at the Pentagon."

He balanced the pencil between his hands and Mercedes thought about how fragile the tiny piece of wood appeared against his strength. He didn't realize that in those same hands, he held her heart, her very life. He didn't have a clue that he could snap her in two just as easily as that pencil.

"I already know about the job. Lex told me."

Dammit, she thought, Lex never could keep his mouth shut. There was no telling what her brother had added or taken away from the facts. He'd always had an irritating way of relaying information as he saw it. And what the hell was he doing telling Gabe about it, anyway?

"I'd have a great salary," she went on. "A cushy office. A big staff to do my bidding."

He shrugged as his gaze dropped to the desktop. "Sounds like a dream come true."

Stung by his indifference, she asked, "Is that all you can say?"

Without looking at her, he rose from the chair and walked over to the coffeepot. "What do you want me to say?" he asked as he splashed the strong liquid into a foam cup. "I wish you the best. I hope you'll be very happy in D.C."

The fact that he could so easily assume that she was leaving the Sandbur, leaving him, was enough to send fury ripping through her. Instantly, she marched over to him, snatched the cup from his hand and slammed it down on the table. "You might know exactly how to treat a horse, Mr. Trevino, but you damn sure don't know about handling a woman," she said tightly.

His black brows pulled together in a puzzled frown, which only infuriated Mercedes more.

"What is that supposed to mean?" he questioned. "I'm trying to be nice about this and—"

"Nice! You think I want nice?" Groaning with frustration, she threw up her hands. "You've got to be the most thick-headed man I've ever met!"

His jaw clenched. "Look, if you came over here thinking I'd start begging and pleading for you to stay, then forget it. We both know that your leaving is—for the best."

Mercedes had never thought she possessed much of a temper. She might be feisty, but she never got angry. Not raging angry as she was now.

"You really believe that?" she asked through gritted teeth.

Turning his back to her, he muttered sharply, "I have to believe it!"

Catching him by the arm, she tugged him around to face her. "If that's the way you feel, then I've made a big misjudgment in you. I thought—" She struggled to swallow as tears began to burn her throat. "Deep down I thought you were capable of loving—of loving me. But I can see now that you're only concerned about yourself. That I've been no more than a passing distraction to you." Unable to bear touching him for another second, she jerked her hand away from his arm. "You're no different than the bastard who broke my heart eight years ago! Which only proves what a bad judge of men I am!"

Whirling away from him, she started to leave the room, but his hand caught her shoulder. The touch of his hand on her bare skin sent streaks of fire racing up and down her arm.

"Maybe you ought to explain that," he demanded in a steely voice.

Biting down on her lip, she slowly turned and met his gaze. "Eight years ago, the affair I told you about was with one of my professors in college. At that time, he vowed that he loved me and wanted to spend the rest of his life with me. I began to plan a future with him, blissfully unaware that he'd just happened to leave out the part where he was already married," she said bitterly. "So don't be using Sherleen as an excuse to shut me out of your life! I know what lies and rejections and betrayals are all about, too! The only difference between you and me is that I was foolish enough to fall in love again. And this time, it's with a man who doesn't even possess a heart!"

Gabe stared at Mercedes in stunned silence, trying to understand what she'd just said, when she let out a choked cry and ran out the open doorway.

Part of his mind yelled at him to run after her and stop her a second time, but the other part of him was paralyzed, incapable of moving a muscle.

Mercedes had fallen in love with him? Is that what she'd said? That she *loved* him?

His hands shaking, he sank into the desk chair and dropped his head into his hands. All along, he'd convinced himself that she was only playing with him, that a few nights of sex was all she wanted or needed from him. It had been easier to let himself think in those terms, easier to keep his heart at a distance. Or so he'd told himself.

Yet the moment Lex had told him about Mercedes's job offer, a part of him had died, withered like a weed in the desert. And he'd known that he'd been fooling himself all along. He loved the woman. He'd just been too afraid, too proud to tell her so.

And now he was on the verge of losing her. He *would* lose her if he didn't do something, and quick.

Dismissing the call he'd promised to return, Gabe hurried out of the barn to find her.

Twenty minutes later, after stopping at her office and finding it empty, then calling the big house to discover she wasn't there, either, Gabe moved on a hunch and headed back to the horse barn.

Before he entered the cavernous building, he met one of the grooms wheeling out a wheelbarrow full of manure.

"Eddie, have you seen Mercedes anywhere around the ranch yard in the past half hour?"

"Sure have. She left a while ago on that roan gelding."

Anger and fear rushed through Gabe. He'd warned her about riding that horse, but apparently she'd decided his opinion didn't count for much. "You mean, the blue roan—Mouse?"

Eddie took off his straw hat and scratched the top of his head. "Yeah, that's the one. He's as mean as a snake, if you ask me. But she seems to love him. Makes you wonder what women are thinking sometimes, don't it?"

Yeah. Like how she could love him when he'd been as mistrustful as Mouse, Gabe thought ruefully.

"I'd better go look for her," he muttered more to himself than to the groom, then hurried toward the barn door.

Eddie called after him. "Want me to saddle a horse for you, Mr. Gabe?"

Gabe waved a dismissive hand back at him. "No. I'll take care of it."

Five minutes later, he was galloping away from the ranch yard, directing his horse toward the west and the river, a route that he knew she loved to ride. It took him an hour to reach the banks of the San Antonio, but he didn't get so much as a glimpse of her or even Mouse's tracks. And the way back to the ranch was just as fruitless.

Once he unsaddled, he made another visit to Mercedes's office, but it was dark and empty. When he tried the big house again, Cook informed him that she hadn't seen Mercedes since she'd left early that morning.

Feeling frustrated and angry at himself for not coming to his senses sooner, Gabe decided the only thing left for him to do now was wait for her to return and hope that she would be willing to forgive him.

The rest of the afternoon passed at a snail's pace for Gabe. Even though he kept himself busy with a pen of yearlings, he found himself looking up every few minutes, hoping to see Mercedes riding back into the ranch yard.

Where was she? What was she doing? Was she out there sulking somewhere, determined to make him worry and fret? No. Mercedes wasn't purposely mean. She wouldn't want to deliberately hurt him—even out of anger. Dammit, why hadn't he realized that weeks ago? It was something he'd be asking himself for a long time to come.

When sundown came and Mercedes still hadn't appeared, Gabe could only make one conclusion. Something had happened to her.

After giving orders to the wranglers, he punched in Matt's number on his cell phone while he headed for one of the ranch's pickup trucks.

He hated to call the man, but Lex was off the ranch on business today, and Matt was more than the general foreman of the ranch, he was Mercedes's cousin, one that was very nearly like a brother. But Matt's first wife had been killed when she'd ridden a spirited horse away from the ranch. Gabe realized Mercedes's disappearance would only bring back bad memories for the man, but finding her was the most important issue now.

"I rode out earlier today to find her," he explained a few moments later as he related the facts to Matt. "I didn't see her anywhere, but then she could have taken a different trail."

"Let's not panic, Gabe. She could have ridden in an entirely different direction."

Gabe swallowed as fear threatened to overtake him. If something bad had happened to Mercedes, he'd never forgive himself.

With the phone still to his ear, he started the truck and gunned it out of the ranch yard. "She's on Mouse. I told her not to ride him—he's totally unpredictable. But she—well, she was angry with me. She probably rode him out of spite."

A grim silence ensued and then Matt said, "Yeah. I know all about an angry woman," he said ruefully. "But Mercedes can ride probably better than you and me put together. I have to believe she's all right. I'll get some of the hands together. We'll saddle up and fan out over the place until we find her."

"Good. I'm heading toward the river again," Gabe told him. "I'm still thinking she went in that direction."

He snapped the phone shut and drove onward across the rough pastureland. After a half mile passed, he suddenly spotted Mouse loping out of a grove of mesquite trees. The empty saddle on his back caused Gabe's heart to take a nosedive and he was forced to clench the steering wheel to keep his hands from shaking.

*Oh, God,* he prayed. *Don't let her be injured. Don't let me lose her like this.*

When the horse noticed the truck, the animal instinctively ran toward it. Gabe stomped on the brakes and jumped out at the same time Mouse trotted up, seeming relieved to finally see a human.

"Whoa, boy. You're all right now," he said soothingly as he latched on to the dangling bridle reins.

The horse was sweating and dancing in a nervous jig. Gabe had to struggle with him for a couple of minutes before he was able to examine him and the saddle. A quick inspection showed no blood or sign of injuries. The lack of evidence should have given him a tiny amount of relief, but it only worried him more. Something had made Mercedes fall. But what? And where was she?

Trying to keep himself calm so that he wouldn't spook Mouse even more, he carefully tethered him beneath a nearby hackberry tree, jumped back into the truck and called Matt's cell number again.

"I've found Mouse," he blurted without preamble. "He's fine, but no sign of Mercedes. I've tied him along the trail. You'll find him when you head this way. I'm going on to search for her."

Gabe tossed down the phone and stepped down on the gas. Unless Mouse had been wandering around in circles, Mercedes had to be close by, he thought desperately.

Fifteen more agonizing minutes passed before he spotted her walking on a cattle trail, heading toward the ranch. He tromped on the gas and the truck bounced wildly over several fire-ant hills until he finally reached the spot where she'd halted on the beaten track.

By the time Gabe braked the truck to a stop and rushed to her side, he was so weak with relief, his legs felt close to collapsing.

"Mercedes! My God, look at you! Are you hurt? What happened?"

Her white shirt and blue jeans were covered in dirt, her straw hat bent into an unrecognizable shape. A bloody scratch across her cheek had dried to a brown mark, but otherwise she appeared safe and sound. She was staring at him as though he were the last person she expected to see, which only made Gabe feel even worse about the things he'd said to her.

"I'm fine," she said in a weary voice. "I'm just ashamed to admit that I got bucked off."

Groaning loudly, he grabbed her by the shoulders and tugged her into his arms. As he buried his face against the side of her hair, he gently scolded, "Mercedes, I told you that Mouse was an outlaw! I told you not to get on him!"

Mercedes suddenly realized he was trembling with fear. She wrapped her arms around his waist and pressed her cheek against his chest in an effort to reassure him. He'd been searching for her, she thought incredulously. He did care for her. He had to!

"It wasn't his fault," she reasoned. "We came upon a rattle-snake in the trail and it struck at Mouse's front leg. Before I could get control of him, he began bucking. I landed in a patch of hedge roses and Mouse ran off. I had no choice but to start walking."

"Damn horse! I found him back up the trail." He eased her away from him and shook his head. "Mercedes, when I saw that horse running across the pasture without you, I was—terrified."

Yes, she could hear the aftermath of his fear quavering in his voice, see the concern on his face. It stunned her, thrilled her, to think he might actually care that much. "I'm sorry, Gabe. I never meant to worry you. After this morning—"

"Mercedes," he blurted before she could say more. "This isn't the time or place, but I don't give a damn if we're stand-ing in the middle of a cow trail. Everything I said this morning was a bunch of hogwash. I don't want you to go to D.C. I don't want you to go anywhere. I love you. I think I've loved you from the moment I danced with you that first night we met. I was just too damned afraid, too proud to admit to myself that I could ever need anybody in my life again. Instead, I tried to convince myself that you were the same sort of rich, conniving woman Sherleen had been. And—"

"Oh, Gabe," she interjected, "I'm not anything like her—"

"Wait. Just wait a minute and let me explain," he gently countered. "You're exactly like your mother. Strong and independent. You don't need a man to take care of you—"

"But, Gabe—"

He held up a hand to thwart her protest. "I can live with that, Mercedes. But after we made love, you never bothered to tell me how you felt about me, about your job, about anything that was important to you. What was I to think? That you didn't care? That you didn't want to share that part of your life with me?"

Tears brimmed from her eyes and spilled onto her cheeks. "I've been afraid, too," she whispered as she reached up and clasped his dear face between her palms. "And I'm sorry, Gabe. I should have talked to you—really talked to you. But I'm—you see, for the past eight years, my job has been keeping secrets. The importance of keeping the simplest details to myself was constantly pounded into me by my superiors. And—" She dropped her gaze from his and swallowed hard. "Once I didn't do that and paid serious consequences for it. Since then, I've become—well, not very good about expressing myself to others."

"Can you tell me about it now?"

She looked up at him and tried to smile through her tears. Yes, she could tell Gabe now. Because finally, finally she'd learned to trust again.

"To make a long story short, I became close friends with a fellow airman. His name was Drew and he was a funny, charming guy that I liked immediately. We both worked in intelligence, but I was one security level higher than him. Time went by and I was beginning to think he was a man I could become serious about. And since I'd had a heck of a time getting over John, this was a big step for me. Apparently Drew must have sensed that I was growing fond of him, because he ultimately used that fondness to pry classified information from me."

"I'm so sorry."

"Yeah. So was I. Sorry that I'd been so foolish as to trust him. Especially when I knew better. He went straight to my superiors with the information, and though it wasn't any data that would have caused serious harm, it was enough to tell them that I couldn't be trusted. The whole thing made me look like Mata Hari and Drew like 007."

"What a bastard."

"No. I don't blame him. I was the one at fault. For trusting him in the first place. For opening my mouth when I should have kept it closed." Her arms tightened around him, and this time when she smiled, her eyes were smiling, too. "But I'm not in the military anymore. And I don't have to guard my heart anymore now that I've found you. You're going to be so sick of me telling you every little thing that you'll probably want to drag out the duct tape," she teased.

"I should be apologizing, too, Mercedes. I wasn't exactly being open and honest with you. I guess we've both got a lot to learn about trust."

Sighing with relief, she said, "If you'd not jumped to conclusions so quickly this morning, I would have told you that I have no intentions of going to D.C., or anywhere else. Now or ever."

His fingertips gently wiped at the tears on her dusty cheeks. "Do you really mean that?"

"Oh, Gabe, I went riding this morning in hopes that it

would calm me down. I was so angry with you because you didn't seem to care. I kept asking myself if it might be better if I took the job in Washington."

His eyes were sober as they roamed her face. "And how did you finally answer yourself?"

"The answer was easy," she softly replied. "The Sandbur is where my heart is. Here with you. Besides, deep down I'm a cowgirl, and that's all I ever want to be. And your wife. If you want me."

Tender awe filled his gray eyes as he stroked a hand over her tangled hair. "With me, Mercedes, what you see before you is all you get. Is that enough to keep you by my side, to give me children?"

Love beamed from the smile that spread across her face. "What I see before me is enough to last me a lifetime and beyond, cowboy."

He swept off her hat, then bent his head to kiss her. Mercedes clung to him tightly, letting her lips convey all the love in her heart.

Finally lifting his mouth from hers, Gabe grinned. "Matt has a posse out looking for you. We'd better get back to the ranch and let everyone know you're safe."

They started to the truck, and with a happy chuckle Mercedes curled her arm around the back of his waist.

"And I'd better call Mother and tell her that she has a wedding to plan."

Suddenly concerned, Gabe glanced at her. "What do you think she's going to say?"

Laughing, Mercedes leaned over and kissed his cheek. "That it damn well took us long enough."

\* \* \* \* \*

*Turn the page for a sneak preview of*
AFTERSHOCK, *a new anthology*
*featuring* New York Times *bestselling author*
*Sharon Sala.*

*Available October 2008.*

# n●cturne™

*Dramatic and sensual tales of paranormal romance.*

## Chapter 1

*October*
*New York City*

Nicole Masters was sitting cross-legged on her sofa while a cold autumn rain peppered the windows of her fourth-floor apartment. She was poking at the ice cream in her bowl and trying not to be in a mood.

Six weeks ago, a simple trip to her neighborhood pharmacy had turned into a nightmare. She'd walked into the middle of a robbery. She never even saw the man who shot her in the head and left her for dead. She'd survived, but some of her senses had not. She was dealing with short-term memory loss and a tendency to stagger. Even though she'd been told the problems were most likely temporary, she waged a daily battle with depression.

Her parents had been killed in a car wreck when she was twenty-one. And except for a few friends—and most recently her boyfriend, Dominic Tucci, who lived in the apartment right above hers, she was alone. Her doctor kept reminding her that she should be grateful to be alive, and on one level she knew he was right. But he wasn't living in her shoes.

If she'd been anywhere else but at that pharmacy when the robbery happened, she wouldn't have died twice on the way to the hospital. Instead of being grateful that she'd survived, she couldn't stop thinking of what she'd lost.

But that wasn't the end of her troubles. On top of everything else, something strange was happening inside her head. She'd begun to hear odd things: sounds, not voices—at least, she didn't think it was voices. It was more like the distant noise of rapids—a rush of wind and water inside her head that, when it came, blocked out everything around her. It didn't happen often, but when it did, it was frightening, and it was driving her crazy.

The blank moments, which is what she called them, even had a rhythm. First there came that sound, then a cold sweat, then panic with no reason. Part of her feared it was the beginning of an emotional breakdown. And part of her feared it wasn't—that it was going to turn out to be a permanent souvenir of her resurrection.

Frustrated with herself and the situation as it stood, she upped the sound on the TV remote. But instead of *Wheel of Fortune,* an announcer broke in with a special bulletin.

"This just in. Police are on the scene of a kidnapping that occurred only hours ago at The Dakota. Molly Dane, the six-year-old daughter of one of Hollywood's block-buster stars, Lyla Dane, was taken by force from the family apartment. At this time, they have yet to receive a ransom demand. The housekeeper was seriously injured during the abduction, and is, at the present time, in surgery. Police are hoping to be able to talk to her once she regains consciousness. In the meantime, we are going now to a press conference with Lyla Dane."

Horrified, Nicole stilled as the cameras went live to where the actress was speaking before a bank of microphones. The shock and terror in Lyla Dane's voice were physically painful to watch. But even though Nicole kept upping the volume, the sound continued to fade.

Just when she was beginning to think something was wrong with her set, the broadcast suddenly switched from the Dane press conference to what appeared to be footage of the kidnapping, beginning with footage from inside the apartment.

When the front door suddenly flew back against the wall and four men rushed in, Nicole gasped. Horrified, she quickly realized that this must have been caught on a security camera inside the Dane apartment.

As Nicole continued to watch, a small Asian woman, who she guessed was the maid, rushed forward in an effort to keep them out. When one of the men hit her in the face with his gun, Nicole moaned. The violence was too reminiscent of what she'd lived through. Sick to her stomach, she fisted her hands against her belly, wishing it was over, but unable to tear her gaze away.

When the maid dropped to the carpet, the same man followed with a vicious kick to the little woman's midsection that lifted her off the floor.

"Oh, my God," Nicole said. When blood began to pool beneath the maid's head, she started to cry.

As the tape played on, the four men split up in different directions. The camera caught one running down a long marble hallway, then disappearing into a room. Moments later he reappeared, carrying a little girl, who Nicole assumed was Molly Dane. The child was wearing a pair of red pants and a white turtleneck sweater, and her hair was partially blocking her abductor's face as he carried her down the hall. She was kicking and screaming in his arms, and when he slapped her, it elicited an agonized scream that brought the other three running. Nicole watched in horror as one of them ran up and put his hand over Molly's face. Seconds later, she went limp.

One moment they were in the foyer, then they were gone.

Nicole jumped to her feet, then staggered drunkenly. The bowl of ice cream she'd absentmindedly placed in her lap shattered at her feet, splattering glass and melting ice cream everywhere.

The picture on the screen abruptly switched from the kidnapping to what Nicole assumed was a rerun of Lyla Dane's plea for her daughter's safe return, but she was numb.

Before she could think what to do next, the doorbell rang. Startled by the unexpected sound, she shakily swiped at the tears and took a step forward. She didn't feel the glass shards piercing her feet until she took the second step. At that point, sharp pains shot through her foot. She gasped, then looked down in confusion. Her legs looked as if she'd been running through mud, and she was standing in broken glass and ice cream, while a thin ribbon of blood seeped out from beneath her toes.

"Oh, no," Nicole mumbled, then stifled a second moan of pain.

The doorbell rang again. She shivered, then clutched her head in confusion.

"Just a minute!" she yelled, then tried to sidestep the rest of the debris as she hobbled to the door.

When she looked through the peephole in the door, she didn't know whether to be relieved or regretful.

It was Dominic, and as usual, she was a mess.

Nicole smiled a little self-consciously as she opened the door to let him in. "I just don't know what's happening to me. I think I'm losing my mind."

"Hey, don't talk about my woman like that."

Nicole rode the surge of delight his words brought. "So I'm still your woman?"

Dominic lowered his head.

Their lips met.

The kiss proceeded.

Slowly.

Thoroughly.

\* \* \* \* \*

*Be sure to look for the* AFTERSHOCK *anthology next month, as well as other exciting paranormal stories from Silhouette Nocturne.*
*Available in October wherever books are sold.*

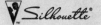

# SPECIAL EDITION™

Tanner Bravo and Crystal Cerise had it bad
for each other, though they couldn't be more
different. Tanner was the type to settle down;
free-spirited Crystal wouldn't hear of it.
Now that Crystal was pregnant, would
Tanner have his way after all?

**Look for**

# HAVING
# TANNER BRAVO'S
# BABY

by *USA TODAY* bestselling author
## *CHRISTINE RIMMER*

*Available in October wherever books are sold.*

*USA TODAY* bestselling author

# Merline Lovelace

*Undercover Wife*

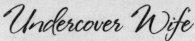

Secret agent Mike Callahan, code name Hawkeye,
objects when he's paired with sophisticated
Gillian Ridgeway on a dangerous spy mission
to Hong Kong. Gillian has secretly been in love
with him for years, but Hawk is an overprotective
man with a wounded past that threatens to
resurface. Now the two must put their lives—
and hearts—at risk for each other.

*Available October wherever books are sold.*

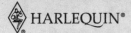

# REQUEST YOUR FREE BOOKS!

## 2 FREE NOVELS PLUS 2 FREE GIFTS!

# SPECIAL EDITION®

## Life, Love and Family!

**YES!** Please send me 2 FREE Silhouette Special Edition® novels and my 2 FREE gifts (gifts are worth about $10). After receiving them, if I don't wish to receive any more books, I can return the shipping statement marked "cancel." If I don't cancel, I will receive 6 brand-new novels every month and be billed just $4.24 per book in the U.S. or $4.99 per book in Canada, plus 25¢ shipping and handling per book and applicable taxes, if any*. That's a savings of at least 15% off the cover price! I understand that accepting the 2 free books and gifts places me under no obligation to buy anything. I can always return a shipment and cancel at any time. Even if I never buy another book from Silhouette, the two free books and gifts are mine to keep forever.

235 SDN EEYU   335 SDN EEY6

---

Name                                    (PLEASE PRINT)

---

Address                                                                     Apt. #

---

City                              State/Prov.                    Zip/Postal Code

---

Signature (if under 18, a parent or guardian must sign)

Mail to the **Silhouette Reader Service:**

**IN U.S.A.:** P.O. Box 1867, Buffalo, NY  14240-1867
**IN CANADA:** P.O. Box 609, Fort Erie, Ontario  L2A 5X3

Not valid to current subscribers of Silhouette Special Edition books.

**Want to try two free books from another line?**
**Call 1-800-873-8635 or visit www.morefreebooks.com.**

* Terms and prices subject to change without notice. N.Y. residents add applicable sales tax. Canadian residents will be charged applicable provincial taxes and GST. Offer not valid in Quebec. This offer is limited to one order per household. All orders subject to approval. Credit or debit balances in a customer's account(s) may be offset by any other outstanding balance owed by or to the customer. Please allow 4 to 6 weeks for delivery. Offer available while quantities last.

**Your Privacy:** Silhouette is committed to protecting your privacy. Our Privacy Policy is available online at www.eHarlequin.com or upon request from the Reader Service. From time to time we make our lists of customers available to reputable third parties who may have a product or service of interest to you. If you would prefer we not share your name and address, please check here. ☐

SSE08R

# COMING NEXT MONTH

### #1927 HAVING TANNER BRAVO'S BABY—Christine Rimmer
*Bravo Family Ties*
Tanner Bravo and Crystal Cerise had it bad for each other, though they couldn't be more different. Tanner was the type to settle down; free-spirited Crystal wouldn't hear of it. Now that Crystal was pregnant, would Tanner have his way after all?

### #1928 FAMILY IN PROGRESS—Brenda Harlen
*Back in Business*
Restoring classic cars was widowed dad Steven Warren's stock in trade. And when magazine photographer Samara Kenzo showed up to snap his masterpieces, her focus was squarely on the handsome mechanic. But the closer they got, the more Steven's preteen daughter objected to this interloper....

### #1929 HOMETOWN SWEETHEART—Victoria Pade
*Northbridge Nuptials*
When Wyatt Grayson's elderly grandmother showed up, disoriented and raving, in her hometown, it was social worker Neily Pratt to the rescue. And while her job was to determine if Wyatt was a fit guardian for his grandmother, Neily knew right away that she'd appoint him guardian of her own heart any day!

### #1930 THE SINGLE DAD'S VIRGIN WIFE—Susan Crosby
*Wives for Hire*
Tricia McBride was in the mood for adventure, and that's just what she got when she agreed to homeschool Noah Falcon's two sets of twins. As she warmed to the charms of this single dad, Tricia realized that what started out strictly business was turning into pure pleasure....

### #1931 ACCIDENTAL PRINCESS—Nancy Robards Thompson
Most little girls dream of being a princess—single mom Sophie Baldwin's world turned upside down when she found out she was one! As this social-worker-turned-sovereign rightfully claimed the throne of St. Michel, little did she know she was claiming the heart of St. Michel's Minister of Security, Philippe Lejardin, in the process.

### #1932 FALLING FOR THE LONE WOLF—Crystal Green
*The Suds Club*
Her friends at the Suds Club Laundromat noticed that something was up with Jenny Hunter—especially Web consultant Liam McCree, who had designs on the businesswoman. Would serial-dating Jenny end up with this secret admirer? Or would a looming health crisis stand in their way? It would all come out in the wash....

SSECNM0908